PREYS
PERSONIFIED

PREYS

PERSONIFIED

TABLE OF CONTENTS

DEDICATION

This book is dedicated in loving memory of my grandmother, Evadney Victor. You taught me to believe in myself and my voice. You were my staunchest supporter, and I miss you immensely and love you.

To my beautiful daughters Daina and Nyah,
Your presence has made my life so beautiful. All that I do is for and because of you.
You have given me the strength to overcome my fears and take this gigantic leap of faith.
I truly understand the word love because of you.

ACKNOWLEDGEMENTS

In the pursuit of being the epitome of all that I was created to be, I begin these acknowledgements like how I face each day and anything that transpires in my life. First honors go to the President and CEO, the only wise God – Jehovah; to whom be the glory, honor, dominion and power both now and forever. Without whom, I am nothing and cannot do absolutely anything!

To the phenomenal Lilly Morgan, you did not know me, yet took me under your wings at the request of a friend and guided me each step of the way. The world needs more people like you and I publicly applaud you. Your gigantic heart, insightful nature, wisdom and spirituality was what was necessary for Preys Personified and I know beyond a shadow of a doubt that we were predestined for such a time as this. You stood with me when it was 50 pages, edited, proofread time and time again, and suggested different routes to take in my approach to certain aspects. Thank you for keeping your word and being hands on. You are extremely valuable in my world and I owe the success of this book to you.

To the fabulous and amazing Tiffany Knowles, I came to you with the gargantuan request to edit this book in a small window. You did not hesitate in agreeing to do so. You jumped right in and surpassed all expectations and demands made of you. Thank you for your frank remarks and the time you dedicated to this. I appreciate you immensely.

To my fantastic parents, Devon and Evangel Ollivierre, saying thank you seems so small in comparison to all you've done for me. However, I want to publicly acknowledge the pivotal role that you have played in my life. God did an excellent job (as always) when He chose you to be my parents. You took this duty to heart ensuring that my physical, emotional and especially my spiritual needs were met. The disciplines as a child were never appreciated, but as an adult, I would not be who I am without it. To say that, I love you would be an understatement. I am because you are.

My amazing siblings Latoya and Sharonique Ollivierre! Appreciations to you for always rooting for and believing in me; for being my sounding board when I was uncertain, and scared and nervous about this project or life experience. I love you immensely.

It is often said that cousins are a girl first friends and I am thankful for my amazing cousins Shavernell Hoilett, Nalisha Edwards and Rocina Hector. You have fought for me, counselled me, prayed with me and stood with me through some of the darkest and brightest days of my life. Having you in my corner make life interesting and easier to maneuver.

To Tais Gonzalez, Eustecia Herman, Jeffrey Duroseau, Daisha Henry, Onica Stewart and Joy-Ann Davis. Thank you for taking the time out of your busy schedules to read the book in its entirety and give your honest critiques. I know you have adopted some of the characters as your own, seeing yourselves in them and you're rooting for others (lol). Your input made editing easier to do. I appreciate your help in shaping it into the awesome project it has become.

My "Take-the-roof-off" friends Samantha Forrester-Smith, Alexander Joseph and Peradeba Raventhirajah, you jumped onboard to help make the first cover of Preys Personified come to life. Thank you for believing in the dream and aiding in making it a reality. Sammy, you kept pushing me, stating if you don't like it, change it until it is what you want, and you never gave up on me. You believed in the vision from the inception and made sure that I didn't quit. I am truly blessed to have you in my corner. You rock, hun!

To those who have prayed for me when I couldn't pray for myself, walked with me through mountain top and valley experiences, gave me the unfiltered truth when it was essential, supported me and my ministry in any way and have just been there for me with a prayer or an encouraging word, thank you! My heartfelt gratitude to you. Without you, none of this would be possible.

Lastly, but certainly not least, my beautiful amazing daughters - Nyah and Daina – you are the reason why I do all that I do. You have kept me grounded, focused and determined through some of the lowest stages of my life. God in his infinite wisdom knew what he was doing when he blessed my life with you.

Darlings, there is no limit to what you can do and be. You do not have to be defined and constrained by others' opinion of you. The world is your global village and you have the gifts, anointing and favor of God to take you anywhere the mind can dream and your heart can conceive. All you have to do is believe that you can do it, and it can and will be done, because I certainly believe in you. Infinity is your limitation.

Only DO What Your Heart Tells You

Princess Diana

CHAPTER 1

Victoria hated coming to The City. It seemed that everywhere you turned you were bombarded by throngs of scantily-dressed women, either in person or on the gigantic screens filling the area. Sex was used to sell everything, even aspirin! She was very vocal about her dislike, too, and her friends could hardly understand why. They would look at her like she had an extra eye growing out of her forehead whenever she was hesitant about taking a trip into Manhattan.

"Not like The City?! You must be mad, Vicky!" one friend had bluntly retorted once. People flew millions of miles just to experience the excitement of New York City. "The Big Apple," "The City That Never Sleeps" — it was the place where everything happened. You could be all that you wanted to be and then some. It was the melting pot for every race, creed, ethnicity and language of the world. One friend said, it has that certain *je ne sais quoi* that no other place in the world had, and to actually live so close to it - just a train ride away - and never experience it for all it has to offer was "such a tragedy." Eventually, her friends stopped inviting her out whenever they decided to go - which seemed to be every weekend.

To be honest, she didn't mind the non-invitations. Actually, she was fine with it. It meant she would not have to fabricate a reason for her absence anymore. Just as her friends thought she was weird, she too found their obsession with The City bemusing. There was absolutely nothing appealing about it to Victoria. In The City, it seemed like everyone was always in a rush. You couldn't walk two blocks without bumping into someone. You're poked and pushed without so much as an 'excuse me,' and when you do say something, you draw angry stares or swear words. It was loud and noisy. What's more, a constant feeling of anxiety cloaked her whenever she went there; like at any moment, she was going to be run over by one of the million yellow cabs that flew by and honked aggressively because you were crossing the street too slowly for their pleasure. It wasn't that The City didn't have its charming side, it was just that most of the hurtful things that she had experienced in her life were, in one way or the other, associated with that place.

A few months back, Victoria's friend Andrea, had, in her lilting Indian accent, politely but sternly checked her after yet another one of her whining sessions about New York City.

"No one asked you to move here, Victoria!" Andrea scolded her passionately. "You can leave at any time, and go to another state or any other country of the world. No one is holding you hostage. It is your choice to stay here. So, stop moaning about how bad New York is. It is bad everywhere. Trust me, I know!"

Andrea was born into the lowest caste system possible in Kolkata, India. She moved to New York when she was 22, enrolled in college, landed a job as a nurse and never looked back. She wanted to forget everything about her life before she stepped foot on American soil.

For the first two years after her arrival, she worked day and night, without taking a vacation, holiday or a personal day. Every penny she earned, she saved until she was content that she had earned enough to never again experience the depth of hunger, despair and poverty that she had endured as a child in Kolkata.

Knowing from how far she had come, Victoria couldn't refute Andrea's argument. She had made a fairly comfortable life for herself, despite all that she had gone through. She knew a lot of people had it much harder than she did, but New York was her training ground and battlefield. She hoped that, at the end of the day, she would win the war that raged against her soul in this city.

****

Victoria didn't know why Richard asked her to meet him on a Saturday morning, in Manhattan. Everyone knew of her disdain. She was dreading it already. Yet, this morning was different. First off, she didn't have to take public transportation. She was pampered and chauffeured in style the entire way into The City, causing her to float on cloud nine. She looked around at the luxurious interior of the limousine with wide eyes. There were chocolate-covered strawberries sitting next to her on the seat of the limousine. Rose petals stood out against the plush white carpet, inviting her to take off her size eight Jimmy Choos and run her perfectly manicured feet right through it. She purred at the softness and left her shoes off for the whole journey. Across from her, dripping with condensation and rising out of the depth of the double-walled, insulated, grey ice bucket, was a giant bottle of unopened champagne with a note that said, "Drink me." She dare not touch it. She knew it would take her entire month's salary just to pay for it, should she open it. Additionally, she was not much of a drinker. She didn't know what was going on but it couldn't be good. Stuff like this didn't usually happen to people like her and she wanted to have all her faculties about her should there be any more surprises.

After what seemed like hours, the limo pulled up to the curb. Victoria hustled to put her shoes back on before the door opened. Just as she finally slipped her feet in, the door opened and Richard leaned in with the biggest smile she had ever seen on him. He kissed her softly on the cheek, while he growled "Good morning, beautiful."

She smiled and said "Good morning."

"Ready?" Richard asked.

"As ready as I can be with all the mystery going on here," she replied sarcastically.

Richard laughed heartily at her comment and escorted her from the confines of the car. Victoria stood still, looking around, getting her bearings and trying to figure out where she was. She was stumped. She did not recognize anything. Seemingly, she had never been to this side of Manhattan before. She laughed at herself. Honestly, she didn't know much about Manhattan outside of Union Square, 34th Street and Time Square. So, her ignorance was no surprise. However, from the looks of the environment and the lack of dog poop on the sidewalk, it had to be one of the more upscale neighborhoods.

Richard placed her hand in the crook of his arm, and escorted her briskly through the foyer of a hotel. Victoria caught a glimpse of herself in the ceiling-to-floor mirrors that lined the hallway and smiled. She didn't do too badly. In fact, if she admitted it, she cleaned up rather nicely. The forest green bodycon dress hit her mid-calf. It accentuated her curves without revealing anything except the fact that she was all woman. The red matte lipstick that she wore popped against her flawless skin. She had pulled her hair in a bun atop her head and finished off the look with gold hoop earrings. Her face was flawless. Her Cinderella six-inch clear whole shoes gave her the height that she would not normally have had and made her stride feminine and purposeful.

Yassss, girl! You are beautiful just like God meant for you to be, she said to herself and turned her attention back just in time to hear Richard say, "You are drop dead gorgeous today, baby." She smiled and kept in stride with him as they made their way down the magnificent corridor.

There is no real beauty without slight imperfection

James Salter

CHAPTER 2

The room she now sat in was stunning! There was no doubt about that. Richard made sure of it. Its beauty held her captive as she gazed around at the decor. Even to her untrained eyes, she knew that all the furnishings in the room were costly. Whomever they had hired to make this place as opulent as it was actually knew what they were doing and had done a masterful job in conveying that. Everything gleamed brilliantly, yet it exuded a charm that was irresistible and very homey. It made you almost forget that you would need two months' salary just to have brunch here. She wasn't accustomed to this sort of extravagance - she liked nice things, and her lifestyle was quite comfortable but she was also a simple island girl. She knew how to live within her means and wasn't trying to keep up with the Joneses. She had learnt from watching her parents early on in life how to work hard for what she wanted and, in whatever state she found herself, to be content until things or her situation changed. Therefore, she worked hard and persevered no matter what, and covered all of her hopes and dreams with much prayer.

Victoria was the Caribbean girl chasing her dreams in the United States of America, the land of opportunity. Still, she never forgot the lessons of her quaint childhood upbringing. She didn't have what her mother called a "red eye." It meant she wasn't envious of what other people had. She was a huge believer that the world was big enough for everyone to prosper and that with hard work and frugality, she could afford to live a lavish lifestyle — if she wanted one. But she didn't. She had a nice enough nest egg stashed away, should the unfortunate events of life decide to darken her door. She would not be hopeless or helpless again. She would be able to make it for a good two years and not really worry. However, the grandeur of this place had her eyes widen with wonder. *Maybe she could afford to step up her lifestyle a bit?* The fact that she wasn't much of a morning person wasn't helping her circumstance either. Her equilibrium was certainly thrown off today. This was a whole new experience that made her feel unlike herself, and she didn't like feeling like this. She was the girl that was always in control. The one that ran the board meetings; the one that everyone came to for help, advice or just to unload the cares of their day. She usually had a solution for every problem that her friends encountered. She was the Oprah amongst her friends, solving all of their problems, either with financial assistance or sound advice. She had not always been this way, though. Life had indelibly transformed her into the altruistic creature that she was today.

Victoria had left her tiny island of Mustique to pursue her dreams of becoming a doctor in America. She was such a naive, young girl then. She thought that people would be kind, open and caring to those from her Grenadine island, but the "concrete jungle" had eaten her up and spat her out, too many times to mention. She had abandoned her dream of becoming a surgeon and replaced it with one of survival. She learnt the hard way to fend for herself, and not trust that everyone had the best of intentions. She was no longer the guileless girl that left the isle over ten years ago and, though she had an aura of innocence about her, she was very astute and wise beyond her years. New York could do that to you. You grow up fast after the initial culture shock. You learn to put your head down and work hard to avoid homelessness during the winter. You learn to smile without meaning it. You learn to stand up for yourself, to barter, to negotiate, to use your voice, lest someone to take advantage of you.

She made a promise to herself many years ago — that one day she would write her autobiography. She would tell the story of her struggles - her way, *from princess to pauper to independent New York businesswoman*. It would be a bestseller. Of that, she was quite certain. Life had the best content any author could want and, in her 35 years, she had quite a few tales to tell. Very few people were privy to her woes, and how she had pulled herself up by her bootstraps, but she was certain that there were others who would be able to relate to her struggle. Even more, she hoped that it would help someone thrive in a similar situation because, though she struggled violently at one time, she ultimately overcame and survived. She hoped she could help many avoid the vicious pitfalls she had encountered. Her father always said, "stretch back your hand and help those that are coming behind." It was her duty and privilege to help make life easier for those that followed.

All that glitters is not gold.

William Shakespeare

CHAPTER 3

Victoria looked across the table at Richard, the man who had her in this seat of opulence. She stared at him as the aroma of the blood red roses, which seemed to bloom out of the center of the virgin white table cloth, filled her nostrils, causing the butterflies in her stomach to take flight. She surveyed the room again with her mouth slightly agape. Everything was perfect.

Maybe too perfect, she thought.

The silverware reflected the light softly, causing things to appear as though they were glowing. The crystal glasses sitting on the table sparkled like diamonds as the beams from the dome-shaped chandelier reflected through them. A bottle of Dom Pérignon hugged tightly by a dazzling white cloth napkin sat chilling in the ice bucket.

Champagne for breakfast, that's a first, she thought and giggled to herself. If what she thought was about to transpire, she would need a glass of champagne, maybe even two or three.

Richard was everything that she had prayed for — well, almost. He was tall with rugged good looks and ambitious (sometimes to a fault), comical (this hinged drastically on what mood she was in - he had a weird sense of humor), intelligent, had good teeth, and his breath never overwhelmed her to the point of dizziness like some of the other men her friends had tried to set her up with recently. The thought of those men caused imaginary spiders to crawl up her spine and she shuddered in disgust, triggering Richard to ask her if she was okay.

"I'm fine," she answered demurely.

"Yes, you are," Richard said smiling, rubbing his thumb across her knuckles and looking deeply into her eyes.

He didn't know what he had done in his previous life to be so lucky, but he was not complaining about it. Victoria, or Vicky as her friends called her, was one of the most beautiful women he had ever laid eyes on, and that was saying a lot. In his 38 years on earth, he had had his share of women. In fact, he had lost count of the number of women he had slept with, truth be told. He might need to check his black book when he got home to get a ballpark figure. Whatever that number was, Victoria superseded them all in fully capturing his attention.

Victoria was about 5 feet 6 inches, hitting him just above his chest when she was in heels. Barefoot, she was just below his chest, but when she walked into a room, it seemed to shrink in her presence. He liked his ladies slender, between dress size six and eight, but Victoria was nothing of that sort. She was not a petite girl by any degree. She was a size 12 but with curves in all the right places, curves that made your imagination run away with itself, causing you to want to do things only a man with his superb skill set between the sheets could do to a woman so exquisitely made. She by no means flaunted them, but she was certainly "blessed" and knew just what to wear to complement her sexy frame. God had definitely spent a little more time on Victoria in comparison to some of the other women he kept company with and, for that, Richard was grateful.

Everywhere he went with her, he could feel the gazes of all the fellas in the room, following her and undressing her with their eyes, but she never paid them any mind. She always made Richard the center of her attention, like no one else in the world mattered at the moment. This was not new to him. Most women did that for him. They would choose him over the other people in their lives, even friends they'd known for years. He made sure of that. Separating them from what they knew usually allowed them to cling to him and be there whenever he wanted them, at the drop of a hat or the snap of his finger. He liked it that way.

With Victoria, though, this was not possible. From the very beginning, he had tried to guilt her into feeling bad about the fact that she had turned him down when he had asked her out. Rather, she explained she had made prior plans with her friends and couldn't change them at a moment's notice. She stated firmly that her friends and family meant the world to her and, unless he was her husband, there were no two ways about it. Yet, with that established, she never made him feel unwanted. The big deal for him was that Victoria let anyone who approached her know that she was there with someone - not just anyone, but him! She did this without expressing it verbally; it was in the way she angled her body, tilted her head, or just laid her hand softly next to his. She was confident, articulate, intelligent and warm. When she smiled at him, she drew him like a moth to a flame.

He didn't know what it was about her that got to him. *Maybe it was because they hadn't slept together yet?* He was not accustomed to waiting so long for the goodies. Typically, by the end of the first month, most of the women he knew would have already been in his California King Size bed, pledging their undying love to him and getting to "know" him in the biblical sense. He smiled at that thought. If his bedroom could talk, *Oh my! What tales it would tell.* Of course he loved these women! He loved how they made him feel, provoking his body to react voraciously. He was just never *in love* with them. Love was something that you sold to fools, and most of these women were enveloped by the notion. Everyone wanted to be in love or be loved.

A man who carries a cat by the tail learns something

he can learn in no other way.

Mark Twain

CHAPTER 4

Richard Washington smiled to himself as he reminisced on his life and value. Most people saw what he allowed them to see – the philanthropic millionaire, who kept his nose clean. Nonetheless, Richard knew he was a player; he took pride in this on a private and personal level.

He had been that way ever since he had gone from a chunky, pimple-faced kid whose feet were too big for his body into an Adonis amongst men, practically overnight. For his seventeen birthday, his body had finally caught up with his feet, and he went from a measly 5 feet to 6 feet 2 inches in six months. His acne had cleared up and his beard came in. His voice transformed from Alvin the Chipmunk to Barry White and that was when the girls started to flock.

He fondly remembered his first encounter into the throes of passion. Her name was Lisa Acevedo. *Lisa, Lisa, Lisa, my, my, my.* She was a fair-skinned Puerto Rican girl with jet black, silky hair down the middle of her back. She was beautiful and she knew it. She had sparkling brown eyes and a curvaceous form for a 17 year old. He had tried to talk with her several times before but she never paid him any attention. Truth be told, she never even remotely acknowledged him. Then, one day, after his growth spurt, she came over to where he was sitting at a cafeteria table with his best friend Sean.

"Hey Sean, hi Richard. How are you?" she queried.

Sean responded on demand.

"I'm great, Lisa. What are you doing on this side of the fence? People like you don't really come to the not-so-popular table."

"Sean Johnson, you are so funny, always advocating for social justice. You should consider running for class president, you could change the social dynamics of our unfair school system," she said, calmly sitting down at the table and crossing her legs.

Her short white pants rode up on her thighs. Richard caught a glimpse of her butt cheeks and instantaneously thought of the staircase to heaven. He had to fight the impulse to stare. He didn't want to come off as a pervert, but those exposed cheeks were doing something to him. His heart raced and thoughts he shouldn't have had permeated his mind.

"I heard that Richard is excellent in math and I am failing it miserably. I was hoping that he could tutor me," she said, staring at Richard while twirling her hair between her fingers and popping the gum she was chewing at the same time.

"Of course he can tutor you," Sean shot back, resting his hand on Richard's shoulder. "Just say when and where, and he will be there."

Sean continued smiling at her while Richard tried not to look dumbfounded.

"How about tonight at my place? We have some assignments that are due and I don't want my grades to suffer because I did not hand them in on time," she said, still looking innocently over at Richard.

"Sure, that is no problem," Sean said.

Silently, Richard was very happy that Sean was there. He knew he would not have been able to speak to Lisa as confidently as Sean was doing.

"Great! Here is my address."

She took a marker out of her backpack, leaned forward and grabbed Richard's forearm, writing her address. Richard was sure she was going to brand him. Everywhere she touched, his skin caught fire. The V-neck top she was wearing sagged open, showing her cleavage. Richard's mouth dried up instantly and he tried to divert his eyes, but he was spellbound.

"I'll see you around 7 p.m., don't be late," Lisa said, grabbing her backpack and walking away slowly.

Richards's eyes followed her until she was out of sight.

"Well, look at you," Sean laughed uproariously, elbowing Richard in his ribs. "You look like a man in the desert who just caught sight of an oasis."

Sean continued teasing Richard by pounding Richard on the back.

Richard pushed Sean off of him and hissed his teeth loudly.

"Seems like you're going to be a busy man tonight," Sean continued laughingly, wiping away tears.

Richard stared at him, not saying anything.

"I hope by the time you get there, you can speak for yourself because, my brother, I will not be around to be your spokesperson," Sean continued, chuckling as he walked away.

Instantaneously, beads of perspiration broke out on Richard's forehead. He needed to get his act together if he expected to impress Lisa, and not embarrass himself.

He had gone over to her house that night to help with the math assignment as Sean had promised for him. Lisa lived with her mom who was a registered nurse and extremely busy. In fact, she was hardly ever around. Right now, she was working a double shift at the hospital and Lisa was home by herself, unsupervised. And on those nights, Lisa did whatever she wanted.

Upon his arrival, Lisa escorted him to her room where her math book was lying open on the bed. Her room was small but neat. There were numerous posters of Backstreet Boys, NSync and a few other groups that he was not familiar with. Her TV was on, and the movie Blade was showing but it was muted. They had gone over the algebra that she said was giving her problems and he realized that she was a smart girl. Math was definitely not a problem for her. He knew she did not need his help, so there had to be another reason why she had invited him over. The thought had no sooner entered his head when she leaned over and kissed him on the mouth as he reached for the textbook. He froze. He didn't know anything about sex, but he watched enough television to know how things worked. He spent many days and nights locked in his bedroom with a bottle of lotion, his imagination and himself, and now he was finally about to experience the real thing. His heart and private part leapt with happiness.

Lisa definitely knew her way around the male body. This was not her first foray into the land of ecstasy. She knew what she was doing and what she liked. Since he had no clue about the practical aspects of sex, he was more than all right with allowing her to lead while he followed. When Lisa undressed herself and then him, Richard didn't complain. He wanted this to happen and now that it was, he was going to make the best of it. It was not what he expected for his first time, but he did enjoy it. He left an hour later, smiling all the way home. He was now a man, in every sense of the word. He hoped that it wasn't a one night stand. There was so much more he wanted to do and find out and he hoped Lisa was up for allowing him to do so. He was over the moon when she asked him to come by the next day, and the day after that and every opportunity when her mother wasn't home.

Over the next few weeks, they were consumed with having sex as often as they could, sneaking around to be with each other. He was getting better at lasting longer and pleasing her and enjoying himself, as well. He liked her a lot and they were cool, but he was beginning to notice that there were a lot more fine girls than Lisa, especially her best friend Cassandra.

Cassandra had that exotic look, which most women from Nigeria did. Her teeth flashed bright white against her blue-black skin, and her eyes twinkled when she laughed. She was beautiful and confident and that was immensely attractive to him. Was it his imagination or was she always licking her lips provocatively when he was around? Three months after he had hooked up with Lisa, he got his answer. Cassandra approached him one afternoon while he was sitting in the cafeteria studying. There were only a few people there and they were doing what they were supposed to be doing - studying. They paid him and Cassandra little to no attention.

"Richard, how are you?" she cooed, dragging her bright pink pointer nail across the nape of his neck. Goosebumps immediately rose up all over Richard's body.

"I am good," Richard responded, trying to keep his voice normal.

"So I've heard," Cassandra smiled, stroking her bottom lip with her pink tongue, looking him up and down suggestively.

Richard's palm began to sweat and he moved his backpack off the table and onto his lap.

"Where is Lisa? I know you guys are thick as thieves and you don't go anywhere without her."

Richard started looking in the direction that Cassandra had come in from and hoped against hope that Lisa would appear out of thin air.

"She is auditioning for the cheerleading squad, and I wanted to talk to you so I thought this would be as good a time as any to do so," she said.

"Oh ok, what's up?" Richard queried, wiping his sweaty palms on the legs of his jeans.

"Imma get right to the chase. Lisa has been talking about how good you are in bed and it has got me thinking that I want to see if what she is saying is true," she said, plopping herself on the table in front of him.

Richard was in shock. He felt his jaw drop, but was unable to stop it from gaping wide open. Cassandra's laughter reverberated throughout the lunch room as she cackled heartily at his expression.

This had to be a game they were playing on him.

"You must think I am stupid, Cassandra. You and Lisa have been friends for forever and y'all probably came up with this idea to see if I would cheat on Lisa. I'll pass," he said, attempting to rise from where he was sitting. However, her booted feet were now sitting comfortably between his legs. To force his way up would mean revealing to her that he was aroused by her. He did not want that happening, so he sat back down.

"I can assure you that Lisa does not know I am having this conversation with you. This will be just between you and me. Our little secret. I promise," she said, making the cross over her heart. "I don't want to lose my friendship with Lisa any more than you want to break her itty, bitty heart, still, I would like to partake of the goods that she has been bragging about."

Her eyes remained glued to his.

"What Lisa doesn't know won't hurt her and I would like to keep it that way. She is, after all, a great friend, but I heard that you are well endowed and I want to see and experience that firsthand, and not even my love for Lisa is going to stand in my way of that."

She ended, leaning forward, resting her cheek next to his and licking his left earlobe.

The feel of her cool tongue on his ear caused Richard's heart to accelerate rapidly and his nostrils flared as he took in a deep breath. Inhaling that deep was his undoing. Cassandra was so close to him that, when he drew that breath, it dragged her soft and sensual perfume into his nostrils. It assaulted his senses and Richard felt blood rush to his private part. He moaned softly.

"I promise I will make it worth your while," Cassandra whispered huskily when she heard his soft moan. "If you want to take advantage of what I am offering, meet me at my place after school. I have the house all to myself for the weekend."

She placed her soft, moist lips in a kiss on his cheek. She then got up and walked away without a backward glance.

Richard was torn and confused. What if it was a game they were playing on him? If he gave in and got caught, then he would be screwed. However, in his business class, he was learning that scared money doesn't make more money; you have to be willing to take some risks. So, it was in life - if you were afraid to take the risks necessary then you will never know what greatness awaits you out there, or what you are truly capable of doing. He decided then and there he was going to see what Cassandra's proposal was all about.

He had been imagining being with her for several weeks now. It was like the gods were taking his dreams and offering to make it a reality. He would be a fool not to see if there was anything to it. He would worry about the consequences later if this turned out to be an elaborate hoax. If Cassandra wanted to sample him behind her best friend's back, he had no problem with that. After all, there was enough of him to go around and variety was certainly the spice of life.

After school, he called Lisa and told her that he could not make it to the date that they had planned.

"I am not feeling well," he lied over the phone while "coughing."

"What is wrong, baby?" Lisa queried, sounding worried. "I can bring some soup and come to take care of you. I don't mind."

Richard felt bad lying to her, but only for a little bit.

"No, that is okay, babe, I don't know what I have and, if it is contagious, I would never forgive myself if I made you sick."

Richard added a couple of extra coughs for effect.

"Oh baby, you sound horrible, yet so considerate to think about my safety," Lisa said with pity in her voice.

"My mom made some chicken soup. I am going to take that and try to sleep. My phone will be turned down, so I won't hear if you call. I will call you tomorrow. Ok, baby?"

"Okay. Feel better, baby."

Lisa blew a kiss through the phone.

"Thank you, I will," Richard said with a smile. He blew a slightly cough-filled kiss back and hung up the phone.

A smile like that of the Cheshire cat blanketed his face. That was much easier than he imagined. Apparently, he had a gift for subterfuge. He immediately got dressed, doused himself in his best cologne and headed over to Cassandra's house. When he rang the bell, she came to the door in the shortest pair of denim pants that he had ever seen. Half of her butt cheek was peeking out. Her blue black skin glistened as she moved and his fingers itched to touch her. Cassandra laughed at his expression and wiggled her index finger in a come hither motion. He followed like a charmed snake.

Cassandra was a year older and much more experienced than Lisa. He had a lot to thank her for. She was a master at this. He learnt a lot of things from her that night and, in the months that followed, her lessons would forever change his life; taking advantage of a situation was at the top of that list. Pretending to have your best friend's back was just one way to go about that. Sneaking around and never getting caught was a priceless lesson and, of course, the mastery of telling lies was a close second. Lisa never found out about him and Cassandra. He was willing to stake his life on it. If you asked her now (not that he knew where in the world she was), she would probably say that she was the only girlfriend he had dated or slept with in high school and he was cool with that misinformation. He was not one to kiss and tell – well, not unless it benefitted him.

From that day, he never looked back. The ultimate goal for him when talking to, spending his hard earned money on or giving a woman vast amounts of his time and attention was to get her into bed and enjoy her in every possible position. He loved sex. He lived for sex. He would kill and maim for it. He was not ashamed to admit it. That was the one and only reason he did what he did. A woman always thinks that she is "the one," that he will eventually settle down with her, or that she'll be the one to change him into an "honorable man." Nothing could be further from the truth. What one wouldn't do, he found another who would only be too willing under the guise that he was being exclusive with her. He had been playing this game for a long time and he was excellent at it. To those who got their heart broken, he always said to them, "Don't hate the player, hate the game." He just played it better than they did. He was by no means ready to throw in the towel like Sean had done. *He settled down with one woman way too quickly*, thought Richard.

The thought of Sean made him cringe. He felt absolutely betrayed. His best friend could have had any woman on Earth. He was tall, dark and handsome, just what most women like. Women fawned over Sean as much as they did Richard. But, no, Sean had gone back to the islands and fallen in love with a homely, island girl who was really nothing to brag about – well, at least from Richard's standpoint. Nonetheless, Sean was smitten. He could not stop talking about his wife. The way things were going, Richard would need a new best friend with whom to hit the clubs because Sean was now officially whipped.

All things considered, Richard had to up his game where Victoria was concerned if he wanted her hooked. She wasn't falling for the things other women had. He had to make her feel like *wifey*. Just thinking about winning her made him smile. Instantly, he knew what would do the trick. *This next gesture will finally make her give up the goods,* he thought. He licked his lips slowly and continued smiling. Everything was going as planned.

I cannot let you burn me up, nor can I resist you. No mere human can stand in a fire and not be consumed.

A.S. Byatt, Possession

CHAPTER 5

Victoria saw the smile and blushed. Richard had a great smile and he was truly easy on the eyes. With his mocha complexion and greenish-brown eyes, he was a very handsome man. He was a warm person as long as you were not sitting across from him at a boardroom table. He was loving, generous, no baby-mama drama *(praise God)* and confident – sometimes, too confident, the kind that bordered on cockiness. The only thing that Richard wasn't (and may present a problem in the long run) was a Christian; or, as her mother would say, he wasn't "sweetly saved." It was a bone of contention between them since she had known him. He wasn't accustomed to going so long without sex, so their discussion was often centered on the sexless part of their relationship, and that was beginning to gnaw at her nerves. With that being the exception, he never tried to stop her from going to church or practicing her faith. He even visited her church a few times.

Victoria knew that she would need to let him know that this was not a phase, and that she wasn't playing hard to get. This was who she really was. She had done some things in her life that she was not proud of, but after reading Dauren and Joan Francis' book "Dating and Courting with Godly Purpose," she decided to wait until she met and married her husband to be engaged again sexually with any man. It was her responsibility to choose wisely.

She knew that God was not going to drop a man in her lap. He would honor her choice, but she needed to be wise and informed when contemplating her preference in a husband or as her pastor liked to call it, her helpmate. She knew that sex would only distract her from this, and sleeping around only developed unhealthy soul attachments to other people. She had seen firsthand what soul ties did. Her friend Jasmine had gotten caught up in that web and things had spiraled out of control.

Profound sadness enveloped Victoria as she thought about Jasmine. Jasmine had jumped in front of the number 4 train at the Nostrand Ave stop in an attempt to end her life. She found out that her boyfriend of two years, Tyrone, got engaged to someone else after they broke up. It had only taken five months before he asked someone to be his wife. She decided that she could not take life anymore without Tyrone. So, she did the unimaginable.

Victoria had spoken to her the day before the incident and she knew she was a little down emotionally. The sudden end to her relationship with Tyrone caught her off guard and she plummeted into a state of depression for a while. But Victoria never expected that she would do anything like that.

Jasmine was beautiful and intelligent. She was warm, kind and so funny, always looking out for others and it didn't take much to make her happy. She loved baking and cooking. She was always in the kitchen creating some sumptuous dish for her family. Victoria owed her ample shape to many of Jasmine's tasty treats. Any man would have been blessed to have her in his life. And, while many had pursued Jasmine passionately, it was Tyrone she had chosen. Victoria never understood why Jasmine chose him. Whereas Jasmine was kind, sweet and gentle, Tyrone was uncouth, foul-mouthed and downright harsh on the eyes, ears and presence. Victoria kept her opinion to herself and remembered one of her mom's old-world expressions, "Every moldy bread has its cheese," which meant there was someone for everyone no matter what others thought of that person.

The way Tyrone treated Jasmine at the end of their relationship, though, was difficult to watch as an outsider, much less as one of her best friends. Jasmine, however, didn't let much bother her. Yet, when Tyrone abruptly left her, he emptied the bank account that they shared. He scarcely contributed anything to it whilst they were together and had taken everything out of the account. He also took the car that they had bought together, and basically left her penniless and homeless. This last act broke Jasmine's spirit profoundly and she withdrew from the world for a bit. Nevertheless, Victoria thought that she was on the mend; she was talking and interacting a lot more with her friends, even smiling back when people smiled at her. Victoria was helping her get back on her feet. She paid her rent three months in advance so there would be one less thing to worry about. Victoria got her firm to contract Jasmine to cater their corporate luncheons and some major events they hosted that year. Things looked promising and there was no indication that Jasmine was on a downward spiral again.

Victoria was shaken to her very core when she got the news that Jasmine tried to end her life. The miraculous thing about it was that she had failed in her attempt. She was in the ICU at Interfaith Medical Center when her mom told Victoria that she was in a coma. Nonetheless, the prognosis was good. Victoria could not imagine the pain and despair that Jasmine experienced prior to making such a profound decision. Life was difficult but Victoria always believed in the concluding lines of *Desiderata* —"With all its sham, drudgery and broken dreams, it is still a beautiful world."

Every day Victoria visited Jasmine, hoping against hope that she would open her eyes. Each visit, she prayed and talked with her, reminiscing on the fun times they had together. Vicky was trusting that Jasmine was hearing her and fighting her way back to them as much as they were fighting and praying for her.

On one of her visits, she stood, looking down at her beautiful friend lying helpless – so tiny and frail in the hospital bed – and her heart grew heavy as she thought of the remarkable life she could have. Victoria was not giving up, though. She served a God of the impossible and there was a purpose to what was happening here. She knew it! Her God was too loving and kind to allow this just for some warped pleasure. There would be a lesson and testimony that would come from this.

"You were doing so well, Jazzy. What triggered you? What happened that you didn't tell me about?" she asked quietly, tears rolling down her cheeks.

She stroked her friend's hair and spoke gently.

"I'll be back tomorrow, honey, I promise."

She kissed her friend on the forehead and walked out of the hospital, praying that Jasmine would still be there when she visited the next day.

As to marriage or celibacy, let a man take which course he will, he will be sure to repent.

Socrates

CHAPTER 6

Victoria was stressed. On one hand, she had Richard pressuring her for sex, and on the other hand she had her momma wanting grandbabies before she got too old to play with them. If her dad was still around, he'd tell Victoria's mother to leave her alone and let her make up her mind when she was ready. She smiled thinking about her dad. He was a kind, soft spoken giant. He was the reason that she believed that all men were not the same. She knew that there were those who would love and take care of you without breaking your heart.

Her dad had met her mom at age 19 and fell head over heels for her charm and wit. When he heard stories of men treating their wives shabbily or giving them babies but not sticking around, he would say that "those men didn't have much sense." He believed with all his heart that a man could be faithful to one woman all his life, and vice versa.

He always said that a man would even grow to become a better person with the right woman by his side. He said simply, "you just had to have a good communication strategy."

He married her mom on her 20th birthday and celebrated 40 years of love and marriage until the day he died. If Victoria could think of any marriage she'd like to pattern, it was her mom and dad's. Was Richard someone who she could spend a lifetime with?

As it stood, though, Victoria was not ready for either sex with Richard or children demanded by her mom. She wanted a marriage that was filled with love, a mate with whom she could pray, confide in, and rely on to do right by his family, without her having to be his warden. She wanted someone who would be her helpmate in every sense of the word. She wanted a man who would help her raise godly children and not force her to do it by herself. She wanted a man whose passion was the things of God and not one who simply upheld a form of godliness. She knew anything was possible, and Richard had started coming to church with her, but would he be sold out for God? She had her doubts so she was praying hard for clarity and guidance where he was concerned.

To add to the growing list of people stressing her out was her best friend Sarai. Whenever they spoke to each other, Sarai wouldn't let up about Victoria's sexless love life. For Sarai, the idea of celibacy, in her words, was "ludicrous and madness, sheer foolishness and utter craziness."

Once, Victoria invited Sarai to be a part of a pact to practice celibacy until marriage and was met with dead silence. Victoria moved in closer to repeat herself.

"I heard you the first time, Vicky, and HELL TO THE NO!" Sarai exclaimed, getting up and walking around to stand in front of Victoria.

"Nope! No! No! No! I am not going the celibacy route," Sarai emphatically stated, shaking her head vigorously. "Vicky, that is an antiquated position for women to have. In this day and age, females have the same power and authority that men have to do with their bodies what they please."

Sarai was growing even more passionate by the second.

"How would you know what pleases you and what you like if you don't experiment?" she continued, looking at Victoria with a bulldog face.

"Women are expected to remain chaste while men are encouraged to sow their royal oats. Hopping in and out of beds, the way one uses the washroom. I, for one, am not going to listen to some dried up old man or woman telling me what to do. These so-called men and women who are holier than thou now, when they were my age, were doing way worse than I am, but hiding to do so, yet the evidence is quite real by the numerous damaged children they left behind."

Sarai huffed, folding her arms across her chest.

"This is the 21st century. I am not hiding what and who I do. It is my life and nobody's business but my own. I will not be conforming to any of it."

At an early age, Sarai had come across the book *"Souls of my Sister"* by Dawn Marie Daniels and had promised herself never to be a victim of living her life for the praises, love and sake of a man. She desired to be as strong as the women in the stories she had read.

"What if you wait and then marry this man and he doesn't bring you satisfaction in bed? How are you supposed to survive in that marriage?" Sarai asked.

She went on without allowing Victoria to get a word in edgewise.

"Not me! I am not ending up with no man who doesn't know how to work it. Most men go into the bedroom just huffing and puffing for ten minutes, stiffen up, fall off, roll over and go right to sleep, while the woman lays there wondering what the hell happened."

Her voice increased in volume as her passion on the subject took over. Victoria quickly got a retort in.

"But you wouldn't have to worry about that if you *wait* to enjoy just your husband. You will be learning and enjoying each other's bodies without comparing yourself to others. You learn with each other," Victoria responded.

"Vicky, you honestly believe that?" Sarai asked, arching her left eyebrow. She reminded Vicky of Dwayne "the Rock" Johnson when she did that thing with her brow.

"Men say we talk too much, but these men outside here trading stories are worse than we are. Just yesterday, my friend, Davina Stanley… you remember Davina…the tall, thin white girl with the red hair? She is married to Jason, the tall, light-skinned, bald-headed guy with the glasses that works at Richard's company."

Her eyebrow went higher still.

"Yes. I remember her," Vicky said, nodding her head.

"Well, she came crying to me yesterday. Poor child. Apparently, her husband told his friend Norris that she is no good in bed. He's even found someone who is way better than her and is willing to do the nasty things that she's not willing to do. He plans to drop her for this new girl."

As Sarai retold the story, she took a seat across from Victoria.

"Well, during some pillow talk, Norris told his wife Rena, who in turn spilled the tea to her best friend Desiree. You remember Desiree, right?! The short, light skinned girl with the crew cut that is built like a sumo wrestler and has diarrhea of the mouth?" Sarai asked.

Vicky tried hard not to laugh at the apt description of Desiree.

"I remember her but that's not nice, Sarai," Victoria admonished, trying not to laugh.

"You know it's true, I just call it as I see it," Sarai hissed. "Doesn't your Bible say the truth shall set you free? Anyways…!"

She continued, not waiting for a response from Vicky.

"We both know Desiree can't keep anything to herself. You know she went and told Davina?! Now all hell is breaking loose over there. Last report I got was that the cops were called last night. While he was at work, she put all Jason's clothes in garbage bags out on the curb, changed the locks to the house and set his brand new Benz on fire," Sarai informed Victoria.

"Ouch," Vicky said, shaking her head.

"Ouch is an understatement. I always thought Jason was different, that man walked like he couldn't hurt a fly but I guess he falls in the category of most men."

Victoria looked skeptically at her friend.

Sarai went on for another 30 minutes about how his wife was not some little tot on the side of the street selling her favors and how he chose a lying dog like Norris to confide in.

"Norris — of all people?" Sarai said, with an exasperated look on her face. She began pacing the living room again.

"What is wrong with Norris?" Victoria queried innocently.

"Vicky! Norris has a plethora of women that Rena does not know about. That is another soap opera waiting to happen when Rena gets wind of that. We all know she has a few screws loose. However, it's not my business to tell," she said, dusting her hands of the matter.

It was only last week that Norris tried to woo a female bartender at the club where he plays on the weekends. Sarai explained that every time he gigs there, the woman gives him a free rum and coke or vodka and orange juice.

"How do you sell your morals and soul for a free orange juice which you can get in the supermarket for three dollars?" Sarai asked.

Vicky giggled at that one, even though she was trying her best not to encourage Sarai's outrageous rant.

"Sarai, not all men are like this. I hope you know this?" Victoria said, moving closer to her friend. "There are both good and bad men and women. We have to be able to discern them and surround ourselves with the good ones."

Victoria read the dejection in Sarai's body and knew she was reliving some of her past relationships that had ended poorly. Oh, the lies! Victoria knew Sarai hadn't gotten over them as much as she wanted everyone to believe she had. Situations like these hit really close to home for her.

"I have seen this too many times with the women in my circle and that, right there, will never be me! You, of all people, should know this! I introduced you to my brother Nicholas thinking that at least *he* would be different than the rest of them, and he proved to us that he wasn't. I am a woman first and that is why I didn't condone what he did then, and why I am rooting for you and Richard now," Sarai said, looking at Victoria with regret in her eyes.

"It's okay, Sarai. Honestly, I thought Nicholas would have been different, too. You live and you learn," Victoria responded quietly.

There was a twinge of hurt that flashed across her face as she remembered what she and Nicholas had. She truly thought it was something special.

"Just -- thank you for not sharing my life information with him nor his with me. We both have moved on and it is best if we stay out of each other's lives," Victoria stated softly.

"Women, like you I admire immensely, Vicky. I am not letting any man think he is more than me and I am not faking an orgasm in bed to satisfy his tiny ego. If I choose to sleep with you, and you are not doing anything for me, I'm kissing my teeth, getting up, putting on my clothes and walking out of there."

"I am serious though, Sarai. Aren't you worried about getting sex without love?" Victoria asked.

"Who said it is without love? I love how it makes me feel. I enjoy myself and I live my life on my own terms. There are many wives at home who lovvveee their husband, making a kissy face...and what does that get them?"

Again, she didn't wait for a response.

"—Pregnant, barefoot, running after kids, while their husband sleeps with any and everything that walks on two legs. My grandmother used to say, 'The rate these men are going, if you put lipstick on a dog, put a dress on it and put it on two legs, these men will try to sleep with it too.'"

"There is no guarantee that will happen to you, Sarai," Vicky countered, looking at her friend squarely in the eye.

"And, what is the guarantee that it won't?" Sarai rebutted.

"There are no guarantees in life," Vicky said. "You make the choice possible and refuse to put yourself in harm's way like you're doing."

"Hmmm, I will live my life my way. I am young, beautiful, educated, and know what I am about. Having sex, is not that big of a deal."

"Yes, it is!" Vicky retorted. "Each person you sleep with, you form a soul tie with them. There is that spiritual connection with them. A soul tie can let a person influence or manipulate you even if they are unaware they are doing so. God didn't create sex to be an audition for dating, or for how good you can turn up in bed and gratify yourself and your partner. Sex is a privilege only for marriage. These soul ties you form can sabotage your future relationships. It is real and it is very serious, Sarai."

"Vicky, you worry too much. I know what I am doing and I will be just fine. I am not letting any man dictate my life. You go ahead and save yourself for your Boaz. I pray you find him soon, though, because those eggs are going to start drying up, and I would love to be an aunt someday," Sarai concluded.

Victoria doubled over in laughter, falling to the floor. Sarai snickered, helped Vicky up, hugged her then left, claiming she was late for a meeting. Vicky shook her head still trying to catch her breath. Her friend was crazy in the best way, but she would keep praying that God would change her heart.

Women need a reason to have sex. Men just need a place.

Billy Crystal

CHAPTER 7

Victoria had come to the conclusion that, of late, there seemed to be an obsession with sex within her circle. Her second best friend, Brittany Leonard, had joined the celibacy pact, or so she thought. Lately, though, any time Vicky brought up the pact, Brittany found an excuse to disappear. A few weeks ago, Victoria finally cornered Brittany after church. She was shocked to learn that Brittany was not keeping the pact that they had made. She thought that if anyone would, it would be Brittany. They both confessed Christianity, attended the same church and Brittany was director of the mass choir. As stunned as she was, she was happier that Brittany had come clean about what she was facing in her life and Christian journey.

Vicky asked her, "Doesn't it bother you that you are engaging privately in sex while publicly professing something entirely different?"

"Yes it does; well, a little bit. It used to bother me much more before, but God and I worked it out, well I hope we did. Plus Christopher wants us to know each other intimately before we get married."

"Wait…what?! You're getting married? And who is Christopher? Why does that name ring a bell?" Victoria queried, trying to catch the fluttering epiphany that floated outside her reach.

Brittany laughed heartily.

"No, I am not getting married. Well, not right now. But we have talked about it." Brittany said, smiling broadly.

"Oh?! Ok. Seems like I have been missing a lot." Victoria said. "How come I have never met this Christopher person?"

"Oh, you know Christopher and you see him all the time," Brittany said laughingly.

"I have?" Victoria probed.

Brittany's right hand mimicked the up and down sign as if one was playing a keyboard.

"Oh, that Christopher!" she exclaimed, the light bulb going off in her head.

Christopher was the keyboardist at their church, and from where she sat he seemed to be a devout and God-fearing man.

"You guys are doing the horizontal polka?" Victoria asked.

Brittany doubled over in laughter.

"Horizontal polka? Who speaks like that? Vicky, you are such a prude," she said between giggles. "Yes we are sleeping together.

Christopher is the best thing that has happened to me in a long time. I don't want to lose him because of not wanting to have sex."

"But, Britt, that isn't right. Proverbs 1:10 says "*My son, if sinners entice you, do not consent. In chapter 3 of the same Proverb, it says trust in the LORD with all thine heart; And lean not unto thine own understanding.* Have you consulted God about Christopher? Have you asked God to reveal his heart and ways to you? Do you think he is a man after God's heart?"

"No, I have not done any of those things, Victoria," Brittany sighed exasperatedly.

"He is a Christian. He is always in church and speaks in tongues. Plus the Bishop would never have placed him in the position he is in if he was not a man of God. God will honor whomever I choose."

Victoria looked at Brittany with eyes wide open in amazement.

"You did not consult God about him? That is a huge mistake, Brittany. Lucifer was an angel, too. There are people that masquerade as children of the light, yet are wolves in sheep's clothing. Even Jesus told the parable of the wheat and the tares, when the farmers sowed the wheat and at night the enemy sowed the tares, and they grew up looking a lot alike. You could not tell one from the other. Jesus had to allow them to grow together until the day of harvest. Only God can show you Christopher's heart. Your emotions are too heavily invested in this for you to see clearly," Victoria pleaded with her.

Brittany folded her arms across her chest, looking at Victoria without saying anything. Nonetheless, Victoria continued.

"You have to think about these things, Britt. You are the mass choir director, people look at you differently and look to you as a role model. You are supposed to be different for these young people," Victoria admonished.

"I didn't ask to be choir director! I certainly didn't ask to be anyone's role model! I have my life to live and I am going to live it unapologetically, regardless of what you church folks think," Brittany retorted angrily, her smile vanishing abruptly.

"That may be the case, Britt, but when you accepted God, you made those choices. We are to be different from the world. Unblemished, and unspotted. The bride of Christ. This is one of the reasons why a lot of young people are turning away from the church. There is no difference and no standard. Nothing to differentiate between the world and us. We are supposed to be lights on the hill, drawing people to the kingdom of God by what we do and say and how we behave," Victoria argued.

"You have your belief, Vicky, and I have mine. Stop being so self-righteous!" Brittany countered, walking off.

Victoria hurried after her.

"Am I self-righteous, because I am not condoning what you are doing? We go to the same church, Britt. We believe the same thing! I am your friend and I should be able to tell you when you are going wrong, especially when so many souls are tied to the decisions that you make."

Brittany shook her head in annoyance as Victoria climbed daintily onto her soapbox.

"I can't tell you what to do but I hope that you will come to your senses because if Christopher is making you choose between him and God, while professing to be this chaste and devout individual, there is certainly a lot more that he isn't telling you, Britt. "

Vicky was willing to stake her life on what she just uttered.

"You know what, Britt? Do what you think is best for you. You always do this, when someone is pointing out something that is wrong with the choices that you are making. I hope for your sake that this doesn't come back to bite you," Victoria said then turned and went back the way she came.

****

Victoria was brought back to reality when she heard her name being called. She smiled across the table at Richard and shook her head in the affirmative in response to his question of whether or not she was okay all while trying to swallow a forkful of the fluffy omelet that she had ordered for breakfast.

"I want to ask you something," Richard said, while reaching into the breast pocket of his jacket.

The omelet turned to cardboard in her mouth.

Oh no, please God, don't let it be what I think it is, she begged silently.

Richard bent his 6 feet-two-inch-frame so that he could kneel.

No, please God, no! She screamed internally, her eyes darting around.

"I know that we haven't known each other for a very long time, but I can't stop thinking about you. You are the first person I think about in the morning and the last when I go to bed. I miss you more than my PS5 when you are not with me. I always want to be in your presence. Your smile makes me feel like I can do and be anything," he uttered lovingly.

He opened the black velvet box that he held in his impeccably manicured hands, and revealed the platinum ring with a black diamond that winked mischievously back at her.

"Would you do me the honor of being my wife?" Richard asked.

The hand that held and softly caressed hers was no longer that of Richard's but of the one that had fed her chicken soup when she was sick. It was the hand that reached across the space that separated them in the car to intertwine their fingers, fingers that matched perfectly and ones she never, ever wanted to let go. The hand that stroked her face tenderly at numerous traffic lights. The hand that reached across to hold her against the car seat for a stop that was too sudden. The hand that hugged her and made her feel like she was the only girl in the world. The hand that had stolen her heart for infinity and ruined her for all other men.

Vanity, wounded pride, rejection, self-delusion. I could recite a litany of little pinpricks that finally produce a gaping wound. That's how marriages and friendships come apart.

Helen Van Slyke

CHAPTER 8

This is not happening, she thought as she looked in the mirror.

The woman in the mirror was someone she didn't recognize. The 5-feet-six-inch frame of the lady looking back at her was draped in a strapless crème mermaid gown with gold threading, giving it an ethereal look. It emphasized how truly beautiful a creation the dress and the woman that wore it were. The dress hugged her like a second skin, highlighting the curves of her size 10 body. She had lost a lot of weight in the last couple of months. It was not intentional but neither was it a bad thing. It had only highlighted her flawless form. Her brown complexion glistened like silk in the sunlight and played peek-a-boo with the shadows in the room. Her dyed, medium brown hair was pulled back in a tight bun at the nape of her neck revealing an oval face that, prior to being made up, had one gasping for breath at its perfection. Now, expertly made-up, it was impossible for one not to take a second look.

Almond-shaped eyes that change color according to her mood peered from the mirror back at her, searching her face. Today, they were plain brown, revealing to an observant person who knew her well that all was definitely not right in her world. Her satin breast heaved as she gulped for air trying to drive back the sudden panic attack that assailed her and caused her stomach to clench into knots. Nausea overcame her. Beads of perspiration appeared on her forehead, disturbing the otherwise flawless perfection. Her left hand reached to dab her brow and the ring on her ring finger caught the sunshine and twinkled impishly, hurdling her back in time.

"Vicky, would you marry me? I couldn't bear it if I didn't have you in my life," Richard said.

Now, everyone was really looking at them. The silence in the room was deafening. The ticking of the clock could be heard across the room. Under the scrutiny of so many eyes, Victoria felt like she didn't have a choice. To say no to Richard here would be to emasculate him in front of so many people.

Maybe I can say yes here and afterwards tell Richard how I really feel, she thought.

She heard herself say, "Of course I will marry you, Richard."

The restaurant erupted in applause causing the crystal champagne glass to vibrate with the impact. Richard rose to his feet, grabbed her and kissed her soundly on the mouth. He pulled her from her seat into his arms and twirled her like she weighed nothing at all. The applause grew louder at his antics and some people came over to congratulate him as soon as he put her down. The men pounded him on his back and offered him compliments on his beautiful choice. Richard smiled, showing off his $5,000-set of pearly whites. He was in his element, the center of attention.

It was at times like this that she was happy she was a black woman and no one could see the blush that spread from the root of her hair all the way to her chest.

"I love you so much," Richard whispered after everyone had ended their congratulations and returned to their breakfast tables. "We are going to be so happy together, babe."

She smiled without it reaching her eyes. She had never imagined herself being married to anyone other than Nicholas. At the thought of his name, her heart skipped a beat and a smile curved her lips. Her eyes turned hazel brown and left Richard gasping for breath as her oval face came alive.

I can't believe I am so lucky, he thought as he stared at her.

He never got used to her beauty. It was not the beauty that the media bragged about. It was a beauty that was ethereal, unconscious and warm. There seemed to always be a glow about her, which either intensified or diminished slightly according to her mood. He'd never encountered anything like it. He always dated beautiful women, that was his norm, yet they never affected anything other than his wallet and body. That was until he met Victoria. He knew he was upping his game, hoping that the ring would have her lower her guard and she would sleep with him. She refused to give up the booty and he couldn't understand it. She was making him work for it. It had been eight months and she still wouldn't budge.

The first time he laid eyes on her, he knew he had to have her. Their paths crossed at a benefit function her company was hosting. It was to raise money to provide free immigration services for undocumented persons. He was the main speaker for the event. He was also certain this prestigious position was due to the one million dollar donation he had made. Victoria's boss was doing the rounds of introducing him to the other speakers. Upon introduction to Victoria, his heart had started beating really fast and everything else slowed down for him. She was his central focus - as prey was in the eye of an eagle. He watched her lips as she spoke to him, yet not hearing anything she was saying. He was caught up in the vision of him tasting those lips. She shook his hand and he felt electricity coursing through his body and into his loins. He crossed his hands in front of him to avoid an embarrassing situation. She smiled at him, said it was nice to meet him and walked away, unaware of her effect on him. He left that night, strategizing the best way he could get her. Over the next couple weeks, he started showing up at her company's office for various things he never bothered with before. He had subordinates that did the day-to-day menial jobs for him. However, he was willing to take over for a bit as his plan required him being in her space, interacting with her more often and gaining her attention and affection.

She didn't throw herself at him like the other women he came in contact with did. As a matter of fact, he didn't seem to exist to her at all. She was polite and friendly whenever she encountered him, but that was as far as it went. She didn't brush into him 'accidently," or drop things and bend over to retrieve them so that he could see down her blouse or up her skirt, as most of the women who tried to get his attention did. He didn't expect to work so hard to get her into his bed. His millionaire status should have at least gotten him to fondle her by now! But nothing! Zip, nada! He knew it was the Christianity thing, and he had tried working around it, even attending her boring church services, but she still wouldn't budge. She had told him that she wasn't going to do that, so if he wanted to leave he could go elsewhere. But he was not going to leave without sampling the goods after having invested so much time and money on her. Hopefully, this ring would change things in his favor. He knew most women gave up the booty after they got engaged, and he was hoping that Victoria would do that, Christian or not. He would get to sleep with her and, after a couple months, he would break it off. However, there was another part of him that wanted to stay close to her, and protect her from the world. This was something new to him.

In all his years of being a "dog," no one had stirred that side of him, with the exception of his mom, and he was wondering if his motives were much more than just sleeping with her. Maybe he wanted more. He needed to have a discussion with Sean about what was happening. Maybe Sean could help him figure this out — after all, Sean had abandoned his black book and become Mr. Family Man.

If you heard Sean tell the story about how he met the "love of his life," you would gag. They had met 18 months ago on a flight. She was on her way to her home island that was a dot on the map - St. Vincent and the Grenadines. Sean was heading to Barbados for the weekend to golf. Instead of going first class like he usually did, Sean had decided to fly coach and experience life as regular folk. That was another thing about Sean that Richard never understood. Why would you work so hard to become wealthy, only to do stuff like that? Enjoy your wealth and let the regular people be.

Apparently, the flight was a full one. Sean had boarded early because their college friend, Mark, was the pilot. He was already seated when Sabrina came aboard and began putting away her luggage in the overhead compartment. Suddenly, she was jostled by a passenger and fell onto his lap. She was so embarrassed and kept apologizing, only to realize that they would be sitting next to each other for the duration of the flight. They then got to talking and talked some more. By the end of the flight, Sean felt like he had known Sabrina for his entire life. That was the beginning of the end for them. Sabrina would spend a month on the tiny island of Bequia, and Sean visited twice during that time. They spoke on the phone every day. When she got back to New York, they were inseparable. Sean asked her to marry him three months later and the rest was history.

Richard had met her several times. She was cool but not his cup of tea, as a girlfriend or a wife. She was always smiling, and talking a mile a minute in her lilting accent. People were drawn to her warmth and fell in love with her charisma. She was fearless, undaunted, and unbothered by the wealth that surrounded her. She was focused on family, spending time with them, God and her faith, and now she had Sean doing the same thing. Sean hardly showed up at the corporate functions anymore and, if he did, Sabrina was a regular staple on his arm. They hardly stayed more than two hours, leaving to go spend time with their six-month twin boys, Colville and Caleb. They were Richard's god children and he loved them dearly. But he couldn't help but curse the day that Sean met Sabrina because that was the end of their bachelor wolf pack.

Homelessness is not a choice, but rather a
journey that many find themselves in.

Asa Don Brown

CHAPTER 9

Victoria twisted the ring around her finger as she paced back and forth in the dressing room of the church. Anyone looking at her would think that it was just a case of pre-wedding jitters. Over the past four months, she tried to come clean and tell Richard she did not want to get married to him but there never seemed to be an opportune time to do so. The first time she tried was when he had dropped her off at the apartment after the proposal but fate decided in Richard's favor. As she started in on the topic, his cell phone rang, and he ran off to deal with an emergency at his company. After that, things just got out of control. As soon as she stepped into the apartment, the telephone kept on ringing with congratulatory messages. This went on for several days. She just couldn't find the right moment to let the cat out of the bag. Family and friends kept calling, wanting the 411 on her engagement and to stop by to see the ring. Most days, she turned the ringer off and let it go to voicemail while she decompressed. Soon, days turned into weeks and the weeks into months. She was at the end of her rope and about to shut the answering machine down for good when she heard the soft, rhythmic accent of her friend Helen, stating, "Victoria, I made it safely. Call me when you get a chance." That message made her smile. It was the silver lining in all of this drama of her so-called life.

It was about a year ago, she was walking to the subway, actually it was more like running to the subway. She was so late for work when she saw this woman, sitting at the station entrance with a cup, asking for help.

"A quarter would do. If you have any food or snacks, I would appreciate it. Anything. Please, anything," she begged.

Everyone ignored her and hurriedly went on their way.

As a regular practice, Victoria tried her best to stop to assist the poor when she could. It was one group of people that would always be among us. Once, she came very close to homelessness herself, so she was sympathetic to the plight of the poor. She took $10 out of her wallet and approached the unkempt lady. She placed the bills in the battered cup held by a gnarled, dirty black hand and turned to walk away.

"Thank you, Miss. May God bless you, keep you and always cause favor to shine on you," the woman responded.

Victoria paused as a sense of déjà vu washed over her. She had heard those exact words many times as a teenager and that voice sounded so familiar. She looked into the woman's face and gasped.

Looking back at her was Helen Deterville, a friend from high school. The bony fist of time had not been kind to her. She looked twice as old as her thirty six years. Her hair was matted and was stuck to her forehead. Her skin was a dirty grey as if it had not felt a hot shower in weeks. Her sunken eyes darted furtively from Victoria to the passersby. Her upper lip was uneven. You could see she had lost half of her upper set of teeth and on both sides of her mouth was something crusty, white and dry.

"Helen?!" Victoria queried.

A range of emotions chased each other across Helen's face. Recognition shone in her eyes and they started leaking. Then, the floodgates broke open, sending a torrent of tears rushing down the various cracks and crevices that lined her face. She tried brushing them away but they would not relent. Victoria reached into her pocket book and withdrew a packet of tissues and gave it to her. Helen grabbed them and tried to mop up her face. Victoria ushered her away from the busy stream of straphangers and made her sit down. She couldn't leave Helen like this. Immediately, she called her job and told them she would not be in today. She didn't know how Helen had gotten to this place. She was one of the brightest students at their school. In fact, she was voted most likely to succeed by her graduation class. After what seemed like hours, Helen was able to compose herself.

"Helen, what happened? How did you get to this place, hun? How long have you been in New York?" Victoria queried, holding tightly to Helen's right hand as she peered into her eyes.

Through Helen's tears, Victoria found out the events that led to her current situation. She had come to New York on a scholarship but after a few months learned that it wasn't enough to cover her living expenses. Being the enterprising young person she was, she had taken a job in a restaurant trying to make ends meet. The restaurant paid foreign students less than minimum wage, but it was better than no money at all; at least it kept her from starving. Initially, she lived in the dorm, juggling work and school. But her grades suffered and she lost her scholarship. She didn't know anyone in New York City besides her classmates and professors. She had built a fair relationship with a girl she met in college named Anna. Anna was friendly and kind to her. The plus side of it was that she was also from the islands, Dominica to be exact, but she had been in New York much longer and knew the run of the town. When the school evicted her from the dorm, Anna took her in, no questions asked. They got separate single beds and squeezed all they had into the tiny space of Anna's room. The other of the two-bedroom apartment was occupied by Anna's roommate - Sheryl and her boyfriend Len. It was crowded, but Helen was grateful to have a roof above her head. She was not out on the street and for that she was immensely thankful.

After the first month, Anna told her she had to pull her weight and help pay for a third of everything if she wanted to keep staying there. That was hard to hear because the little bit of money she was making barely fed her. Nonetheless, she understood where Anna was coming from. Helen was an additional burden that Anna had no obligation to help and was within her right to make that demand.

Helen became frantic with worry and didn't know where she was going to drum up her monthly share of expenses. Her job paid little to nothing, and it barely met any of her needs. Upon her arrival in New York, she was a voluptuous size 16. She was now a size eight. She voiced her concerns to Anna about not being able to make the rent and Anna told her she could get her a job at the nightclub where she worked. Helen didn't know what kind of club it was until she arrived for the interview. It all made sense now — the irregular, late hours Anna kept, the shoe box of singles she had found under the bed once when she was cleaning the room. The minute that Helen walked through the door of the club, her suspicions were confirmed. This was not the kind of life that Helen wanted and she stormed out. She had grown up in a Christian home and couldn't see herself dancing naked in front of men, no matter how hard up she was for money. She had morals and she was not going to let them go. She couldn't imagine what her parents would think if they knew she was doing that.

So, Helen pounded the pavement looking for a job. No luck! To her chagrin, everywhere she went, no one was hiring. Dejected and despondent, she asked Anna to arrange another interview for her. A week later, she returned to the club. It was the shortest interview she had ever done. She was asked two questions. *Can you dance?* To which, she answered yes. *When can you start,* was the next question. She started the same day. With much sadness and embarrassment, she had done what she needed to do to survive. During her performances, she masked her face with the hopes that no one would be able to identify her outside of the club; she didn't want this life following her further than the entrance and exit of that building.

On her calls home to her parents, she never mentioned her plight. As far as they knew, she was living the American dream and was doing really well. Her mom would worry constantly if she knew. She was an adult now, which obligated her to be responsible and accountable. Her parents had done right by her throughout her whole life and had given her every opportunity to advance herself. It would be unfair to ask for help now.

Helen began to add up the liabilities that came with her unsavory New York City lifestyle. One day, after losing her scholarship, struggling to make ends meet, hardly having enough to eat on a daily basis and being forced to strip to keep a roof over her head, Helen had had enough. She came to the conclusion that New York was just not for her. She hated having to fight and struggle all the time. So, she set her sights on saving every penny she could to book a one-way ticket back to her island. All she needed was three hundred more dollars and she could kiss the Big Apple sayonara. One more big nightly tipper was all it would take. She was beyond excited at the thought of immersing herself in turquoise water with the sun kissing her all over. Oh, how she was anticipating year round sunshine again and a warm reunion with her family.

Early one morning, she left the club with a pocketful of cash and in deep thought about how close she was to her goal. She would be reunited with her family in a short time, and she was so excited about it. As she walked down the lonely Manhattan street, she daydreamed about what it would be like to once again stroll through her village market. She loved the smell of sweet mangoes mingling with the sweet morning air. She was paying no attention to her surroundings, since after all she had taken this route so many times before. Unbeknownst to her, one of the guys had followed her out of the club. He cornered her in the alley.

"Hey, beautiful!" he yelled from behind her.

She almost jumped out of her skin because she didn't know anyone was behind her.

"I like how you work it at the club, baby," he continued.

She didn't think anyone knew what she looked like once she stepped off the stage. How did he know who she was? She sped up, her heart in her throat. She could hear him quicken his pace and then she felt him grab her arm.

She recoiled, twirling around and snatching her arm from his grasp.

"Let me go!"

"Oh, you are a fiery one," he said laughing out loud. "I like my women fiery, you will definitely do."

He started rubbing his hands together and licking his lips, whilst looking her up and down suggestively.

"I am not your woman!" she snapped, trying to back away from him. "Why are you following me?" Helen probed.

"Because you are beautiful and I want you to dance for me only. You are definitely my woman tonight. I've been watching you for a while now. Dancing all sexy and then not speaking to people once you leave the club, like you are better than everyone else. Come put some of that uppity behavior on me," the man said, smiling and advancing toward her again.

"Then, you pay for that at the club," she said, backing further away from him.

"How about you give it to me for free?" he said, his smile vanishing.

He lunged for her, wrapping his arms around her waist and dragging her to the ground with him.

"Let go of me!" she yelled, striking him across the face and chest with her pocketbook.

"Help me! Somebody, help me!" she screamed, trying to reach for the mace she carried in her jacket pocket. She never thought that she would need it, but it couldn't hurt to carry it with her. Her mom's mantra was it was better to have it and not need it, than to need it and not have it. Tonight she needed it desperately. Her fingers gripped the mace.

"Shut up!" he spat, boxing her in the face. He followed up with a punch to her stomach. The mace fell from her hand to the pavement and rolled away into the darkness. Helen tried to find it in the dark with one hand, while she fought him off with the other.

"Stop fighting!" her assailant said, punching her again, this time in the face.

The salty taste of her own blood quickly filled her mouth.

"This is happening. You need to roll with it. If you stop fighting, it won't be so painful, you might actually enjoy it," he said with a feral grin, while he tried to unbutton her top.

"Nooooo!!!!!!" Helen screamed. "Let me go!!" twisting her body to get from beneath him.

He straddled her and punched her repeatedly in the face. Helen coughed, trying not to choke on the blood and teeth that filled her mouth. She spat, expelling whole and broken teeth.

"Look what you made me do, mess up that pretty face of yours," he said, shaking his head, while he ripped her shirt open, exposing her breast to the cool night air.

"Stop!" she sputtered between breaths.

"Somebody, please help me," she cried, tears mingling with the snot that flowed freely from her nose.

He bent over her, and in the dimly lit space, Helen caught a glimpse of chiseled cheekbones and feral eyes. He smiled sadistically and a mouth full of gold teeth stared back at her. He grasped one of her breasts and squeezed painfully, leaned forward and brought it savagely to his mouth. He suckled hard and Helen cried out in anguish. She fought to push him away and he bit her. Helen screamed in pain and tried to remove him from her. She fought violently. She would die fighting if she had to. He would not get off easily.

"I said shut up!" the man said, slamming her head into the pavement.

Stars blossomed behind her lids and she gasped for breath. He quickly tore her pants off, and her bare butt hit the pavement. Helen moaned softly trying to shake the fog from her brain. He groped for his zipper, leaning over her. With the strength that she could muster, she dragged her nails across his right cheek, taking a great deal of skin with her. His screams filled the night air.

"You gonna pay for that, you bitch!" he spat with venom and resorted to punching her in the stomach. Knocking the wind out of her, her hands flung to the side. He pulled his pants down and spread Helen's legs wide open. Helen fought violently, kicking at him, and screaming at the top of her lungs.

"No one is coming to your rescue, heifer."

"You might as well lie back and enjoy this," he said, placing his hand around her throat and squeezing.

As he tried to insert himself into her, Helen squirmed feverishly and pulled her body away, while she tugged at the hand wrapped around her slender neck.

"Please God, help me," she pleaded.

"You are making this worse than it has to be. Stay still," the man growled, squeezing her neck tighter.

Helen fought hard between shallow breaths. Darkness was taking over when her hand came in contact with the mace. She kicked at him, pointed the mace at his face and pressed the nozzle. He erupted off her, screaming in pain and swatting at his eyes and nose. He fell backwards on the pavement with his pants around his ankles, swatting at his eyes and coughing.

He fumbled in the dark for a few minutes trying to get up. He got up and pulled his underwear and pants around him.

"I am going to kill you. You're dead!" He wheezed between breaths, firing kicks where he thought she was. Helen crawled away, sobbing silently, trying to get as far away from him as she could without alerting him to her whereabouts. She crawled on her knees in the darkness.

As fate would have it, a young couple passing by heard the commotion and came to investigate. They took one look at the scene and sprang into action. The young woman rushed to her, pulling her on her feet and away from her assailant. She helped Helen to pull whatever was left of her clothing together to cover her body and hugged her fiercely. Helen sobbed in relief. The girl's six-feet-three-inch line backer looking boyfriend rammed his shoulder into the stomach of the assailant, sending him sprawling onto the pavement. He knelt over him, pounding his face to pulp. He stopped, only when the man was no longer moving. During the scuffle between the men, the young lady called 911, and soon the blackened night was aglow with blue and red lights and the air was filled with the piercing noise of the sirens.

Is it possible to succeed without any act of betrayal?

Jean Renoir

CHAPTER 10

Helen spent a month in the hospital. The morning after her assault she woke up with fear's tight fist around her throat. She couldn't see. Her eyes were swollen shut. It took a week and a half before the swelling went down and she could see — albeit as blurry as can be. She smiled satirically as a story from her Sunday school class came back. It was one about the blind man whose eyes Jesus placed mud on then told him to go and wash it off. After the man washed, Jesus asked him what he saw. His response was, *I see men as trees*. She could absolutely relate to him now. It took another week before her sight was completely restored. *Where was Jesus when you needed a miracle?* She had suffered ten broken ribs, a mild concussion and numerous contusions. Anna came to visit almost every day. Everyone at the club missed her and was rooting for her to get well soon. Helen's assault prompted the club to enforce a policy where the girls could not leave without an escort.

Two weeks later, she was discharged from the hospital. She hadn't seen Anna in a couple of days and was a little concerned. Most of her calls, if not all, kept going to voicemail. Helen had hoped that Anna would meet her and bring her home. She knew Anna got busy with extra private party work on the side, and could be gone for days on end. But it wasn't like her to not call. On the day she was released from the hospital, there was no one there to meet her. She got on the bus for the ten-mile ride home. She sat there thinking about how she had narrowly escaped death. She had to make some drastic life changes and do better with the time she had left.

After an hour on the bus, she got off and hobbled to the apartment. She was still sore from the beating she had taken, and areas that were once purple were now regaining their normal color. As she approached her apartment building, a young man who was exiting held the door for her as she limped into the foyer of the building. She took the elevator to the third floor, and inserted her keys into the apartment door, hoping to hear Anna and the other roommate inside, but it was eerily quiet. Usually there would be some type of music coming from the apartment. Anna and Sheryl partied hard so there was hardly any quiet time in the apartment.

She walked into her room and, when she reached the doorway, her heart dropped to the floor. The apartment was empty. Everything was gone, like no one ever had ever lived there. She sped to the vent as fast as her wounds would allow her to move.

"God, please let it be there, please," she pleaded.

The vent was opened and the money that she thought she had hidden so well was gone, and with it, her hopes of leaving the concrete jungle. She felt crushed and plopped to the floor, crying.

"Godddddddd! Why me?! What have I done to deserve this? she screamed. "How could you let all this happen to me? I don't deserve this."

She let out a guttural scream.

Despair pressed down on her and she felt like she couldn't breathe. She cried for hours but it changed nothing. While she was crying, the landlord came in and asked her to leave. The apartment was scheduled to be cleaned and new tenants were moving in tomorrow. Helen questioned how long the apartment had been empty. The landlord informed her that it had been empty for two weeks, and there was no forwarding address given for the previous tenants.

She begged him to let her stay, that she would pay the rent. He asked for an immediate down payment, but she didn't have it. She didn't have a penny to her name. He escorted her out of the building and locked the door behind her. She tried her key, hoping to get back in but it no longer worked. There was no one she could call and nowhere to go. That night, she slept inside the subway car of the "J" train to keep warm. On top of that, with her face mangled and her teeth missing, her job had to let her go, too. No one in the strip club circuit was willing to hire her. She had been optimistic that she would pull herself out, but time had marched on fiercely. That was four years ago. She slept in the park during the summer months. In the winter, she slept inside train cars and any place that kept her out of the bitter cold. She was reduced to begging for a living. Victoria realized that she was crying like a baby with Helen, when she felt tears falling on her hands.

"You are not alone anymore, Helen. I am going to make this right. I'll be here for you," Vicky said.

Victoria escorted Helen back to her apartment and ran a warm bath for her. She added honey-suckled bubbles and helped Helen into the tub. She exited quietly, giving Helen her privacy to relax and soak the months of grime collected on those mean streets away. An hour later, Victoria returned and knocked on the bathroom door. There was no answer. Fearing the worst, Victoria pushed the door open. Helen was sleeping, snoring softly in the bath. Victoria woke her, and sat beside her washing her hair until the water ran from black to clear. She draped Helen in a big, white, terry cloth towel that made its way twice around Helen's frail frame, magnifying how truly emaciated she was. Victoria transferred her from the towel into a plush, purple robe that came all the way down to her calves. She helped Helen blow dry her curly hair and then sat her at the marble-top counter.

Brunch consisted of ripe cubes of mangoes, blood-red strawberries, oatmeal pancakes, Belgian waffles, sausage and eggs. To cap it off was coffee with a hint of cream. She sat in amazement as Helen wolfed down all the fruits and at least six waffles with all of the eggs and sausages. She wondered how a tiny person could hold all that food and not make themselves sick. Helen had cleaned her plate and released a vulgar belch. She looked embarrassingly at Victoria. Vicky smiled and reassured her that it was okay.

After brunch, she convoyed Helen to the guest room, and helped her into a pair of silk pajamas that hung on her like a wet sheet on a line. Helen wanted to know if it would be okay to take a nap and Victoria helped her into bed. Helen fell asleep straight away and began snoring softly. Vicky stood for a bit, watching Helen sleep, tears flowing down her cheeks, then she walked slowly out the room. She checked on her periodically throughout the day. Other than changing positions, Helen was sound asleep. Upon exiting the room after her numerous checks, Victoria leaned against the wall and prayed to God for the strength to help Helen get through the next period of her life.

At 10 p.m. that night, Victoria heard screams emanating from the guest room. She rushed in, flicking the light switch on as she ran in. She found Helen curled up on the floor almost under the bed.

"Helen, it's Vicky!"

But Helen continued to scream. Victoria realized that Helen was still asleep.

"You're only dreaming, Helen. Wake up!" she yelled, shaking her old friend. Victoria tried to wrap her arms around her, so that she wouldn't bash her head against the floor, but she could barely maintain her grip as Helen fought her.

"Helen, I am here, hun. Wake up!" Victoria said as Helen fought to get away from her.

For a tiny thing, Helen was extremely strong. Victoria knew Helen was moving purely on adrenaline, because her eyes were still tightly shut. Whatever she was dreaming about or remembering had her terrified. Victoria laid her gently on the floor and ran into the kitchen. She got a very cold cup of water from the sink and rushed back into the room. She tossed it into Helen's face. Helen's eyes flew open and she came up sputtering. She looked like a deer in headlights. Her wary eyes came to focus on Victoria and her body slumped in relief as realization settled in. She began to weep uncontrollably. Victoria hurried over to her, sat down next to her and wrapped her arms around her as the guttural cries tore through Helen.

Victoria felt her own tears flowing freely as she held Helen. Her wails were soul-wrenching and tore at Victoria's heart. She knew that Helen hadn't told her everything that had happened to her while she was on the streets and, truth be told, she would probably never know all of it. Nonetheless, she would be there for her friend. Whatever she needed, and in whatever capacity, she promised herself. Vicky stayed with Helen all night, alternating between rocking her and praying for her. She prayed like she had never done before, asking God to heal her friend's mind, body and spirit, to give her peace and renew her joy.

Victoria nor Helen saw the light turn from jet black to light gray, then orange. The new day broke through as it had on the day of creation. They had fallen asleep, exhausted by the night's event and the tears that had started the restoration of Helen's life.

The sound of Victoria's phone ringing in the other room woke the ladies. Victoria stretched, trying to get the kinks out of her neck and back. It had been a long time since she had slept on the floor. She remembered that experience like it happened yesterday, though. She was a teenager. Her mom's sister from Trinidad had showed up unannounced. They wanted to surprise her mom because they hadn't seen each other in a while. And what a surprise it was since there were not enough sleeping rooms for everyone. Victoria had to give up her bed and sleep on the floor in the living room at night. They had come to spend a week together and it was the longest week ever for Vicky. She loved her cousins but she was quite happy when they left so that she could get her bed back and not be sore each and every morning she woke up. Before she got up to start the day, Victoria asked, "Can I pray with you Helen?"

Helen was quite reluctant to do so. Truth be told, she told Vicky that she had stopped praying to God a very long time ago. Vicky was sad to hear that and expressed as much.

"Why should I pray to a God that doesn't care about me? God has forgotten about me! He abandoned me!" hurled Helen. "How could the God that my parents taught me about, that I served faithfully all my life, allow me to go through what I did? I have not committed any great act of sin to warrant this? I don't deserve this!

85

With tears falling afresh from her eyes, Helen asked Victoria the next question.

"What could be the purpose for the kind of pain I endured?"

Vicky saw the sadness begin to seep back into Helen as she asked it.

"Helen, I would love to tell you that I know the mind of God where your issue is concerned, as well as why you have been through what you have. To be honest, I don't know why God allowed what He did; however, I can tell you that the God I know is a kind and loving God and He wants the very best for His children," Victoria whispered tenderly.

Victoria quoted from the book of Jeremiah. *For I know the thoughts that I think toward you, saith the Lord, thoughts of peace and not of evil, to give you an expected end.*

"This is not a promise to straightaway release us from adversity or misery, but rather a promise that God has a plan for our lives and, regardless of our current situation, what we may feel, experience and endure, He can work through it to prosper us and give us hope. I know it is not what you want to hear, because your pain is great."

Victoria continued as Helen cried softly.

"Psalm 34:19 says, *many are the affliction of the righteous, but God delivers us from them all.* The righteous face the type of affliction that you have endured. God gives the hottest and most difficult trials to those He knows is strong enough to face, endure and overcome them. Helen, you are in a worthy company. Abraham, Job, Joseph, the three

Hebrew boys, Jesus, Paul and John the beloved are right there with you."

Victoria continued passionately, tears also streaming down her face, as she strongly defended her God in the midst of Helen's despair and doubts.

"They endured unimaginable suffering. It wasn't because they did anything, but it was to get them to the next level in their life and the will of God to be manifested in the world. Nothing worth having comes easily in life. We would love for that to be the case but it isn't. Many people look at their lives through a physical lens but, for us, you and I, and all children that go by the name of Christ, it is so much more. We are spirits being housed in a body of flesh. This body must endure persecution and all forms of challenges and judgments, so we may be worthy of the name that we are called."

Victoria decided to explain how, even though Helen had experienced hardship, she was privileged to practice faith.

"We are able to live and worship freely in this country, and other countries around the world, because many people were martyred to make sure that the gospel could be preached and heard. Our walk is one that is of a higher calling. 3 John 2 says *Beloved, I wish above all things that thou mayest prosper and be in health, even as thy soul prospereth.* You have to believe that God isn't punishing you for something that you may or may not have done. This is not His nature. He is too kind for that. But, I do know this one thing. Your struggles as you know them are now at an end. You, Helen, will be a testimony to many about how and what God has brought you through. I would not be able to tell someone how I survived four years on the street, but you would and you can. I believe with all my heart that in time you will be able to tell them how, even at your lowest moment, God kept you. You should have died in the alley that night, but even then God saved you. It may not have been the way that you imagined but as sure as I am breathing I know God saved and kept you from certain death that night."

Victoria beamed confidently at Helen.

"You are going to look back and see the hand of God all through what you term the worst day or days of your life. You will be able to see that it was still him that was protecting you even as you walked through the valley experiences of your life."

Victoria pressed on, with tears in her eyes.

"Remember the character of Job in the Bible? Job knew that he was upright, that he had not committed any sin, and he held on to that. God thought highly of Job. God allowed everything that Job went through so that he could highlight him to the world. It was the only reason the enemy was allowed to touch his life. Had Job known that 3,000 years later we would be using him as an example of a man of faith, would he have behaved differently? From now on, I want you to remember that," Victoria concluded.

Helen sat there sobbing heavily, snot and tears commingling down her face. Victoria hugged her friend tightly and prayed silently for her.

After what seemed like hours, Helen's tears subsided, and she went into the bathroom. Victoria laid out some of her smaller clothing on the bed for her, called the office and told them she will be out for the rest of the week with a family emergency. She had decided she was going to help Helen feel like herself again. She would have a discussion with her about whether or not she wanted to stay in New York or return home. Whatever she decided, Victoria would help make it possible. She had the means and the ability to do so and she couldn't help but think, maybe this was why God had brought her to the United States, specifically New York. Maybe this was her purpose, to be a light for those who have lost their way and help put them back together.

Helen later decided that she wanted to go back home. She missed her family and she was tired of the concrete jungle. She had seen firsthand how vicious these streets could be and she didn't want to spend her life fighting to make ends meet. Victoria asked her to stay with her for nine months and, after that, she would send her home. Helen agreed to her proposition.

In those months, Victoria took her to the dentist and they fixed her teeth. She took her to the salon for a makeover. She got a new hairstyle, a manicure and a pedicure. She watched as the light of hope came back into Helen's eyes and her body filled out in the months that followed. Helen regained a semblance of her old self. She still slept on the floor next to the bed but the time spent there was becoming much shorter. In month seven, the most amazing thing happened. Helen went to Victoria and asked if they could pray together. Victoria started sobbing uncontrollably with joy. Victoria thanked God for His amazing love and prayed a prayer of thanksgiving. Every day after that, they both made time to pray and study the Bible together. Helen attended church with Victoria and they tried to never miss those meetings. It was there that the word nourished their souls and the company of believers assembled together gave them the strength, joy and purpose to keep going in common faith. Helen was hungry to understand the nature of God and pursued her renewed faith with a passion that rivaled Victoria's.

In the tenth month, Victoria hugged her friend in the departure lounge of American Airlines and watched her walk away. She watched Helen walk down the corridor until she could no longer see her.

I don't need a friend who changes when I change and who nods when I nod; my shadow does that much better.

Plutarch

CHAPTER 11

Victoria's friends meant the world to her but sometimes they just didn't listen. Most times when they turned a deaf ear, it aggravated her nerves and ate away at her patience. She knew the unsavory outcome that came with some of their actions. Nonetheless, she let them follow their own paths and learn from their own experiences.

Take for instance Brittany. Victoria shook her head as she thought about what Brittany was up to. Several weeks ago, Victoria had walked into the huge auditorium ready to be soaked in the water of the word of God. She really needed it at the moment. Her soul had been stained from all the lustful thoughts about Nicholas, the guy she dated before Richard. She hadn't thought about him that often since they broke up but recently he kept popping up in her mind. She had come to church with the full expectation to be washed in the purest, unadulterated water - the Word of God. She sat right beside Britt, close to the front of the stage. Britt had to get there early as the choir director so she always kept a seat for Victoria, who was always rushing from work. Victoria looked around - the over 400-seat auditorium was almost filled to the brim (most of them young adults), mingling and talking, waiting for the program to start.

"Well, well, well..." echoed Pastor James from the entrance of the stage, bouncing into the auditorium, as boisterous as ever. He was the pastor of the local Young Adults Fellowship (YAF).

"Welcome, everyone, I am happy that you are here today. It is going to be a great night and I hope you have come to receive from the Lord," Pastor James said, smiling broadly.

The crowd erupted in cries of amen and applause.

"Let's start this off right. Let's all lift our voices in prayer. "

Pastor James' voice boomed throughout the audience.

All over the auditorium, men and women began to lift their voices in supplication, adoration and reverence. This for Victoria was like coming home. There was no other sound more soothing and pleasing to her ear. She could only imagine how God felt. His word said He lives in the praises of his people, and when his servants prayed it arose as sweet fragrance into his nostrils. She prayed that he was pleased with the worship that was wafting up to him that night. This intensity of worship ebbed and flowed for another five minutes then the voice of Pastor James came over the system with a loud 'amen,' signaling the end of that session. Spontaneous applause and hallelujahs filled the room.

"All right. Let's get started." Pastor James said, clapping his hands together as people found their seats.

"Good evening, everyone. I am so glad you decided to come worship with us tonight. I am really, really happy you did," he said smiling.

"It warms my heart to see my fellow brothers and sisters coming together as one to lift up the name of Jesus. It always reminds me of the Day of Pentecost. I pray that the same experience they had would be ours," he said, placing his right hand over his heart.

Everyone in the building agreed with whistles and a loud round of applause.

"Before we get into the meat of things, I would like to hear your thoughts on the video of Fred Ducas, the popular gospel singer, cursing out the waiter at a restaurant, because his order was wrong. Have you seen this video?" he queried, standing open-legged on the stage with his arms crossed.

There were nods of affirmation around the room.

"What do you think of this?" he asked leaning against the podium for support.

The young lady sitting next to Victoria raised her hand. Pastor James pointed at her and stated, "Go ahead, Ella."

"I think that the behavior he exhibited should not have been done, especially in a public setting. I understand that everyone is fallible and we make mistakes," said Ella. "Someone who is in the spotlight like Fred and a role model for a lot of people around the world, this type of behavior is abhorrent and disrespectful to his faith. I don't know the underlying catalyst for his outburst, but I do know that out of the abundance of the heart, the mouth speaks. Those derogatory and expletives that he issued are a part of him, and he allowed the old man to take him for a ride."

She ended with a bit more attitude and a twinge of judgment in her voice.

"When I saw it, I was very heartbroken, because it made me wonder if there are any more true representatives of God. Are these artists and ministers only portraying Christianity for what they can gain from it?"

"Very good thought analysis, Ella. Thanks for sharing that with us," Pastor James said. "Anyone else willing to share their thoughts?" he queried, pausing for a brief moment.

No one else took up the fight.

"What do you think, Brittany?" asked Pastor James.

Brittany was unaware her name had been called. Her eyes were focused across the room and locked with Christopher's. Vicky followed her gaze. She saw Chris wink seductively at Brittany and the latter smiled approvingly.

What the heck!? thought Vicky.

"Brittany...?" said Pastor James the second time.

Vicky cleared her throat loudly, intentionally, and the day-dreaming Brittany was brought back to reality.

How could they be flirting shamelessly in full glare of Pastor James, unperturbed? Vicky thought hard once more.

Her thought was interrupted as Pastor James began speaking.

"I guess our fearless choir director Brittany is not all here tonight," Pastor James said.

The auditorium erupted in laughter and Brittany shrank into her seat turning beet red. Christopher laughed uproariously.

"Moving on, over the last couple weeks, God has been dealing with me on the topic of sex, youth and the church," continued Pastor James, pacing from one side of the stage to the other. "We live in a society where to begin having sex at an early age is the norm. To not have sex makes you the brunt of a lot of jokes, and more than often most people feel pressured to do it just to fit in. I have been asking God how to address this and he answered in the most amazing way."

He continued, smiling.

"I am here to testify that once God gives you the vision he will make and or make available the provision!"

He clapped his hands loudly and started doing a little two-step dance, which had the audience laughing. It was things like this that made him the beloved youth pastor he was.

"Two days ago, I ran into an old college friend of mine. In college, this young lady was vocal on a lot of issues and in every group you can imagine. I wondered how she found the time to be involved in so many things. Well, that young lady has, as you young people like to say, "blown up" quite significantly. She is now considered the Maya Angelou of coaching young people about sex. She is a certified life and sex coach who leads intellectual men and women of conviction from fleshly frustration into sexual deliverance by educating them using the word of God."

Pastor James watched the audience intently as he continued.

"She teaches people how to embrace and deal with that sexual side of them while still living for God."

Victoria sat there dumbfounded. This must surely be God. Wow! Just wow! Imagine telling God how frustrated you were with the burden of making a decision about sex and, boom, he shows up in this manner.

"Okay, God. I hear you," she whispered, smiling and turning her attention back to Pastor James, as she barely caught his intro line of "help me welcome, this powerful woman of God, Olivia Edwards."

By three methods we may learn wisdom: First, by reflection, which is noblest; Second, by imitation, which is easiest; and third by experience, which is the bitterest.

Confucius

CHAPTER 12

The auditorium erupted in ovation and whistles as the gorgeous Olivia sashayed onto the stage in a blue pinstripe pantsuit. She floated on her six-inch heels as if they were tennis sneakers while dancing to her entrance song of *"Every Praise"* by Hezekiah Walker. She danced around the stage, encouraging the audience to do the same. Her broad, gapped-tooth smile, glistened white. She was beautiful and her smile was contagious. The overhead lights highlighted her orange and black dreadlocks. They fell all the way down her back and swayed with her as she moved. Victoria could understand why she was a sex and life coach. She had the body most women spent a fortune to acquire. Something in the way she moved and carried herself said that it wasn't a surgeon's knife that one should credit. She was born with it.

"I am so happy to be here tonight," she said in a husky out-of-breath voice. "It is such an awesome privilege to be able to speak to you on such an important topic. How could I say no to a phenomenal solicitation to speak on what seems to move the world more than anything else? In addition, I categorically could not say no to my friend Pastor James."

She smiled even more broadly, if that was at all possible.

The crowd erupted with catcalls and screams at the sound of Pastor James' name. He stood, waved and, with hands clasped in front of him, bowed to Olivia. She curtsied and they both smiled broadly. The auditorium exploded in a show of appreciation.

"Ahhh, sex…. the phenomenon that makes people do stupid things," Olivia stated, smiling.

The audience laughed uproariously.

"There is no where we go that we do not encounter the ever-present concept of sex. Even when you come to church. Some churches have even gone as far to say no women are allowed in the front pews because they are a distraction to the men of God seated on the rostrum. My son Gary introduced me to a video by a gospel singer, Stefan Peninsilyn called "Breast, Leg and Thigh." It was basically talking about how women come to church these days. It was a hilarious video - you can check it out on YouTube when you get a chance, and see what I am talking about."

Olivia's chuckle was soon replaced by a deep tone.

"Regardless of the exaggeration of this phenomenon, there are valid points to the argument that the singer addresses. It's the reality of what the church faces today. Other churches have separate seating arrangements for men and women, so there is no distraction whilst in the house of God. We have read about how sex and women have made kingdoms and broken kingdoms."

She continued, becoming even more serious.

"Solomon, the wisest man who ever lived, was stumped by this when he lost his head to the women in his life. Don't go super spiritual on me and think that it was because they stroked his ego. It was because they did a lot more than that. They stroked other things."

The crowd giggled in response.

"Esther was chosen to become Queen of Persia, when she spent one—"

She held up her right pointer finger.

"Just one night with the king...I don't think they sat up reading the Pentateuch either. They were doing things that would make you all blush. The staff of the king spent a year getting Esther ready for that night. She was wearing the best perfume and the best lingerie. The goal was to bring that man to his knees, leaving behind an indelible mark of her presence with him. She left such an impression that one night that he made her queen and, months after, was willing to give her half of the kingdom, and slay utterly anyone who would dare to hurt her."

She roared laughingly.

"My God! My kind of guy! See what the power of a woman and sex can do?"

Olivia continued on with another popular story from the Bible but put a unique spin on it.

"A Moabite woman by the name of Ruth found herself in the genealogy of Christ when she obeyed what her mother-in-law told her to do – that is in Ruth chapter 3:2-5 and also verse 7. She uncovered Boaz's feet, which is a metaphor for sex. As much as we would love to believe the Bible is full of only holy rollers, there are a few characters that didn't begin that way. By no means am I negating righteousness, but I am here to tell you that God will use anyone to get what he wants done. So don't turn your nose down at anyone who did not start off as righteously as you did," Olivia admonished.

Victoria looked around. Everyone was riveted, so captivated by Olivia. You could hear a pin drop throughout the carpeted halls whenever she stopped speaking. The audience was hooked on her words.

"In my line of work, I meet many single women. These women... when you hear their stories....are extremely wounded, acrimonious and incapable of thinking that there is anything good in them, but more so in the men they associate with. They believe that there is no good in any man! One of the common statements is that men are not decent or that all men cheat. They destroy men whenever and however they can! They have no confidence in men, especially when it comes to finding a godly one. Many state that church men are the worst "dogs" there are," she said, making air quotes with her fingers.

"They perpetuate the myth that there are no truly devout men left. Men who can resist the temptation of a good roll in the sack if offered by any woman, regardless of who they are. Therefore, they walk around in their bitterness and claim they are liberated women who don't need a man, save for one thing. And perhaps not even for that either, with the way science is going! What we as the individuals and the church on a whole may not comprehend is that these ladies are just existing with unhealed injuries and are lashing out at men because of the agony the menfolk in their past have poured onto them. Tonight, it is imperative that I be transparent with you in order for the Holy Spirit to do the healing that He wants to do in your life. I want to share a piece of my life story with you. I want to let you in on how I became the person I am today. I know Pastor James told you a little bit about me prior to my arrival - and that was really beautiful - but let me introduce you to the Olivia Edwards that Pastor James wasn't familiar with back then and how she got here.

Olivia clutched the podium with two hands.

"I can say unconditionally and unapologetically that the women I just described, I was one of them."

Victoria and all the other ladies in the room stared intently at Olivia as she began to open up.

"That acknowledgement took me years of counseling to be able to say and not be a hot mess all over this stage. I, Olivia Edwards, was an angry, nasty, man-hater. The funny thing was, I was still trying to get men to shower me with love. Until God stepped in in the nick of time!"

She shook her head knowingly.

"Can I tell you I have been through a lot! I may not look like it for the grace of God but, honey, I have been to hell and back just to stand before you today."

Victoria wondered how deep she'd actually get in the house of God. There have been many visiting preachers who would start with a disclaimer like Olivia's yet, in the end, refuse to share the details of the story that could truly set someone free.

Olivia took a sharp breath in and began.

"My earliest memory was one of abuse. I had been physically ill-treated as a child. Not once, but so many times that I lost count. I watched my mom get beaten. That woman could take a kick and a punch and behave like nothing happened. Oftentimes she was shielding my siblings and I from the rage of our alcoholic stepfather. She was a regular in the emergency room.

Olivia arched her eyebrows and made air quotes again.

"It was always because she was "clumsy."

Olivia waltzed across the stage as she spoke.

"I never understood why she didn't have our stepfather arrested for the assault on her person. I asked her one time, "Mom, why don't you leave?" Her response to me was - "Honey, he is the least of all the evils out there." Today my mom sits in a wheelchair unable to walk because of all the beatings she took at the hands of my stepfather."

Olivia paused. Victoria gasped, trying to swallow the lump that was in her throat. She rummaged through her pocketbook for a tissue to wipe away the tears that were racing down her cheeks and turned her attention back to Olivia.

"When I was sixteen years old, I was raped and sodomized at gunpoint by the boy who was supposed to have my back and be there for me - my boyfriend Anderson. After that experience, I became an even more unhappy and rancorous young woman. Then it became worse. As soon as I got to college, I took it to a whole other level. When men stepped to me, it was "on!" I played the games that had been played on me and I used my body to do so. The minute they fell in love with me, they were out the door. I had the gift of goodbye. I would leave them just like that!" She snapped her fingers for effect.

"I did not look back, did not care what they thought. I delivered that pain the same way it was delivered to me. An eye for an eye! By the time I was a sophomore in college, the notches on my bed were profound. I slept with numerous men. I tried drugs…you name it and I did it. I did it all and I did it well! I was into alcohol and I could drink anyone under the table and back. I did not stop there. I experimented with being bisexual because that is what you do in college to see if women could give you as much pleasure as men did. I flipped between both sexes, trying to fill that black hole inside me. I went on like this for years, using and playing games with men, and besting them at their game while dying on the inside. Why? Because the first man in my life hurt me – my dad. He abandoned my mom and me for another woman. He didn't look back when he left, nor did he support us. My mom got with my stepfather just to keep food on our table and clothes on our backs."

Olivia spoke emphatically, looking out across the audience to check the temperature of the room.

"I didn't have this depth of knowledge at the time, nor was I cognizant that this was the source of why I was doing what I was doing. It would be several years later before I made the connection. Yet, even in that period of my life, unbeknownst to me God was still shielding and covering me."

The auditorium was so still that Victoria could hear people weeping softly behind her. She did not look back as she did not want to invade this private moment of release and restoration that was happening. She was just grateful to be able to share this space with the people she loved. Victoria turned her attention back to the stage as Olivia continued.

"Before I continue with my story, I want to tell anyone who has suffered in any form or fashion to get the necessary help you need from therapy. Yes, you can pray about it! Yes, you can tell it to Jesus. However, God has given you and I the wisdom to know when something is outside of our sphere of expertise. He has also provided professionals in this field to help you get better mentally and emotionally. Get help! Don't be fooled into thinking that it is only for deranged people. Get the support before you go mad. Prevention is always better than the cure and for those who have the disease already, you can still recover if you put the work in."

Olivia started speaking in a hushed tone.

"At the age of 27, I gave my life to Christ. I didn't go to the altar of the church for anyone to pray for me. I didn't even want to go to church that day but I went because a girlfriend of mine kept nagging me to come with her. So, to shut her up, I went with her. I sat there listening to how much Jesus loves me and how He had given His life for me. I heard how there will never be a greater love than His and when everyone fails me He will not! This was what I had been searching for so long. When the altar call was made, I didn't move from my seat. I just sat in the pew, bowed my head during prayer and told the Lord these words, "I don't want this life any more. If you will give me a better life, I will live for you!" No lightning flashed. No voice boomed from heaven, no tingly feeling came over or such. I felt and I knew that I would be different. The past that was holding me hostage was coming to an end."

"Hallelujah! Glory be to God!" 80-year-old Sister Myrtle shouted from the front pew. There was a minute of laughter as Olivia acknowledged her with a huge smile and a little skip and dance.

Olivia went on.

"It was approximately six months after my conversion that I met my kingly hubby. I fell in love with his deep voice and his dimples. He has that Barry White voice that sends goosebumps up and down my spine," Olivia teased while pretending to shiver.

The auditorium erupted in laughter. Some of the guys whistled loudly. She continued smiling.

"Baby!" she said, looking toward the back of the stage. "Can you come out here and meet these awesome people?" she asked laughingly.

Mr. Edwards bounded onto the stage and jogged toward his wife. He was a fine specimen of the goodness of God, Victoria had to admit. He reminded her of LL Cool J with the bald head and dimples. He was tall, much taller than Olivia, and she was wearing heels, so that spoke volumes. He took a bow toward the audience and the auditorium erupted in applause. He smiled and his teeth flashed white against his mahogany skin. His dimples winked impishly. He placed his right arm around Olivia's waist and kissed her fully on the lips. The auditorium exploded with whistles and cheers.

"All right, calm down," Olivia started laughing merrily. "I would like to introduce you to Mr. Kevin Edwards, my priest, my Boaz, my spiritual leader, my covering, my best friend, my lover and father to my children." She looked up at him lovingly.

Mr. Edwards removed his hand from around Olivia's waist, placed it on his heart and bowed before Olivia, then he kissed her again but this time on the cheek. Victoria looked around the audience. There were a lot of broad smiles everywhere.

"I love a lot of things about my husband," Olivia continued, holding on to Mr. Edwards' hand but his love for God and God's word take precedence! I didn't rush into a relationship with him, nor did I push him away, I searched his heart and his mind. I searched my heart and my mind and I talked to God about him...a lot. We got married three years later. I did a lot of praying and fasting when it came to marrying him because most of the nuptials in my family had been unsuccessful and I really didn't have an example of what a good marriage looks like or should look like. But, God was going to use me as the precedent for what a godly, loving marriage would look like."

Olivia's wide smile was contagious. Victoria looked over at the choir stand to see if Brittany was as affected by this love story as she was. She spied Brittany's unchanged countenance.

"There is more to the narrative of my life but that would take forever and I really want to get to this point," she stated matter-of-factly.

"Even though I had been profoundly wounded and even though I more than likely injured many men throughout the course of my college life, God didn't keep a record of that when I accepted him as my Lord and Savior and turned my life around. He sent me a man after his own heart. When I realized this, it blew my mind and made me love God even more. This man that he sent to me helped me through those pains I was still carrying around! God knew I would need Kevin. He knew that not any regular man would be able to bring me out of the place I was in. A lot of my healing and liberation came with my husband by my side before and after marriage."

Mr. Edwards hugged her again around her waist, drew her into him and kissed her on her forehead. Olivia rested in his arms for a brief moment.

Victoria could feel the love emanating between this beautiful couple. She was looking at what a godly marriage should or would look like. She needed her version of that and she was thankful that God was taking the time to let her know it was conceivable. This was why she was waiting.

Olivia took her head off her husband's chest and continued.

"When I say this man bore me up, I am not exaggerating. He stood with me!" she said fiercely, holding tightly to Mr. Edwards' hand.

"I say all of that to say to every single woman who's heartbroken and has a hard time believing men because of the hurt other men have caused them, I comprehend the magnitude of the pain you have endured and are enduring! However, there are godly men still available. There are godly men who follow after God's own heart. There are godly men who will love their wives as Christ loves the church when they marry! You won't have to worry about him stepping out of your marriage for another woman. You won't have to worry about him uncovering you and telling everyone or highlighting your flaws to make himself look good. This man's heart will be hidden in God. He will cover you, protect you, and provide for you and your children. He will be your spiritual priest, your heart will rest safely in him and he will not intentionally hurt you. Why? Because he knows that he will hurt God if he does and he does not want that. He will be your Boaz."

She then turned to look at her husband.

"Thank you, baby, for your presence here tonight. I appreciate you immensely," she said and placed a kiss on his head then watched him walk off the stage followed by a standing ovation.

Olivia waited for the audience to die down. Then, she stated softly, "Ladies and gentlemen, God loves you immensely! So much so that he gave his only son so that you can live and not die. So that you have the opportunity to be the epitome of who he created you to be. 3 John 2 says *"Beloved, I wish above all things that thou mayest prosper and be in health, even as thy soul prospereth."* God wants the best for you. Did I deserve such a godly man? I would say no, not based on my past. But that's not how God is - He keeps no records of the wrongs that you have done. It is not a tit for tat with him, once you have repented. Psalm 84:11, *"For the Lord God is a sun and shield: the Lord will give grace and glory: no good thing will he withhold from them that walk uprightly."* So continue to seek God. Matthew 6:33 says, *But seek first his kingdom and his righteousness, and all these things will be given to you as well.* It is not a lie. It is not a fairytale.

Olivia spoke as if she were pleading with the audience.

"God wants to give you the very best of everything but you have to place him first in all things. Not sometimes, not when it is convenient for you, but at all times. In the daytime, when everyone is looking and the nighttime, when no one can see you. You have to choose Him first in whatever situation you find yourself. In Deuteronomy, Moses knew he was going to die. So he gathered the children of Israel together to admonish them. He told them to serve God wholeheartedly, believe and practice the statutes and commandments given to them. If they serve God, they will prosper and be the head, and they will overtake their enemies. But if they chose to disobey God, then he would punish them and visit their sins unto the third and fourth generations. God is a fair and just God, and He did not choose you to suffer. He can heal your pain and give you a new beginning. He is the restorer. However, in this season of singleness, repent from any iniquity, debauchery, depravity and dishonesty. Pursue God passionately and pray for your healing. Stay focused on doing the work of the kingdom and enjoy being free in the Lord. To the single women who have been broken and wondering if you will ever meet that godly man that you desire, God knows when you are ready and, when you are, He will send you a man that will love you through your storms and treat you the way godly men should treat their wives! And, like me, you will not have to be apprehensive about him using or abusing you. Why? Because he will be a man after God's own heart and men like that want to please God so they will treat you like the Word says they should! I know because I am living proof! To the men who are godly, faithful and have the heart of God, He will give you your Sarah, your Rebekah, in whose bosom you can rest confidently.

Victoria's eyes darted back and forth from Brittany to Christopher to see if they shared any more subliminal communication as if to say, "we need to do better." She couldn't read their expressions well.

As Olivia concluded her presentation, she issued an altar call, encouraging the young and not-so-young to either give their life to God or rededicate their lives to Him. Men and women of all ages and races rushed to the altar. Tears flowed freely down their cheeks. There was hardly any space at all in front of the altar as many knelt, while still, more curled into fetal or prostrate positions before the altar, pouring their hearts out to God. The sounds of worship and weeping commingled in the most harmonious way Victoria had ever heard. Brittany and the choir sang their hearts out as Pastor James and the rest of the youth pastoral team assisted in leading lives to Christ. Victoria didn't go to the altar but she sat quietly in her seat and worshipped, thanking God for speaking to her like her He had. She brushed her cheeks as the tears flowed freely, realizing the front of her shirt was soaked with her tears. She had come expecting God to speak to her and, man, had he! She was renewed to continue doing what she was doing - serving God and being faithful in her waiting period.

People poured out of the door of the church in solemnity. Victoria headed to the parking lot. She was in a state of euphoria after the wonderful experience in the presence of God. On her way to her car, she spied Brittany walking to her car and Victoria hustled to catch up with her. As Vicky neared her, she realized that the Britt was desperately reeling her eyes from coast to coast.

"Looking for someone?" Vicky asked curiously.

"What?!" asked Brittany, jumping and turning toward Vicky. "What the hell are you talking about...?"

"Why are you being so defensive, Britt? I am only asking a question. Are you looking for someone? Maybe Christopher?" Vicky inquired, tilting her head to one side and peering at her.

Brittany glared at her, expecting to hear more.

"What about Christopher...?"

"You tell me," Vicky stated yet again, folding her arms in front of her.

"This thing with Christopher is none of your business, Victoria! Stay out of it! When I want your advice, I will ask for it," Brittany retorted, turning smartly and walking away in anger. She got into her car and sped out of the parking lot, spewing gravel in her wake.

Victoria stood with tears in her eyes. She couldn't believe that she had just fought with her best friend after such an awesome night. Did Brittany not hear anything that was said tonight? How could she leave church unaffected by what just took place? Victoria stood watching the tail lights of Brittany's car disappear down the street. It was normal for the two ladies to get into the business of each other, for, since they first met, many years ago, they had resolved to be each other's keeper when it came to remaining chaste till marriage. Now, all of that had changed. She knew nothing good could come from this, but she was told to mind her business and she would from now on.

Regrets, I've had a few but then again too few to mention. And more, much more than this I did it my way.

Frank Sinatra

CHAPTER 13

Victoria hadn't spoken to Brittany since that fateful night in the parking lot. But about three weeks later, when Victoria saw Brittany's name on the caller's ID, she knew her friend was in need and answered. Brittany was crying hard and it took Victoria a minute to understand what she was saying. Apparently, the way Brittany felt about Christopher was not mutual. A common friend they shared, Wanda, had sent Brittany a video. It showed Christopher and another young lady in a club, so tightly intertwined that air could not pass through them. The video showed them hugging and kissing in the dimly lit room. When confronted, he had no defense except that it was a moment of weakness and that it would not happen again.

"I don't believe him, Vicky. He has done this before," Brittany said between sobs.

Victoria sat, listening as Brittany told her how she had caught him sexting another girl before and had ended things. But he had come apologizing and said it would never happen again.

"I am all yours and no one else's," Christopher stated when Brittany confronted him with the text messages.

She had gazed helplessly into his eyes, eyes that reflected innocence but glittered with something she couldn't quite name. Yet, it made her catch her breath with anticipation - or was it fear? Long, lean fingers caressed her face, causing her mind to blur and what she intended to say was a distant memory. Expensive cologne invaded her senses causing her spine to tingle.

He's mine, she thought.

Her heart danced in her chest and showed through her eyes. She gazed at the man who seemed to have stepped from the pages of *Esquire*. Words of endearment, comfort and persuasion, wrapped intricately in honey that they became inseparable, fell from his lips, barricading the entry for the more sincere suitor who would dare to try and move into his territory. He brushed her cheek lightly and thought it was only a matter of time before she forgave him. As he turned to walk away with her heart in his back pocket, the mask became undone and the deceitful grin appeared.

I still have it, he thought and chuckled.

Brittany hadn't seen any of that, but she had believed and forgiven him and had gone back to him.

It was two weeks after that that Desiree had sent her the video and she felt like a total and utter fool for ever believing him.

"I can't make that choice for you. You told me to stay out of your business, so I am." Victoria cited.

"I know. But I am so confused about what to do," Brittany whined.

"What is the confusion, Britt?" Victoria asked. "You know what you have with Christopher is not real and is not right. Anyone that makes you choose between him and your faith and God, should send up red flags in your mind. This just shows that he is not into you, as you are into him. Walk away, Britt. Don't believe his lies anymore."

"I know you are right, but I am so embarrassed, I fell for his lies," Britt sighed.

Victoria found it very suspicious that Britt had conceded so easily.

"What is going on?" Victoria queried, placing the phone between her shoulder and chin, while she applied lotion to her hands.

Brittany had caught her in the midst of getting ready for bed. She was tired, but she always made time for her friends.

"I don't know how to tell you. I am so embarrassed," Brittany whispered softly.

"Just spit it out," Victoria said, growing impatient.

"I contracted an STD," Brittany stated, barely audible.

"You what?! What the hell?!" Victoria said, almost dropping the phone as her jaw fell.

"I went for my annual GYN check, two weeks ago and my doctor called me two days ago with the result. She says I have chlamydia," Britt said softly.

"The blood of Jesus! Brittany, you had unprotected sex with Christopher?" Victoria asked, stupefied.

"He said that he had never slept with anyone without a condom before, and that he wanted me to be the first because I mean the world to him. He wanted to get as close to me as possible," Brittany said.

Victoria could not believe the girl speaking to her through the phone had a master's degree in education because that was the lamest, dumbest line you could fall for. This girl had no sense, she thought.

"And you believed him?" Victoria queried, struggling to keep the judgement out of her voice.

"No one has ever made me feel like he did. He was always available to talk, and he was there for me. I believed everything that he said," Brittany whispered.

"Brittany, you are lucky it is only chlamydia. That is treatable. You could have gotten HIV. You could have gotten pregnant. Did you think about any of these?"

"Honestly, Vicky, I didn't. I thought he was clean. He actually told me he was and that he had not been with anyone in three years. He professed his love for Christ, so I was sure that he would not do anything to jeopardize what we had," Brittany countered.

"Hmmmm," was all that Vicky could mutter.

"I know… I know and I feel absolutely horrible how I treated you, when you tried to warn me. I am sorry for not paying attention. I know you wanted only the best for me," Britt said apologetically.

"You hurt me very badly, but love makes people do stupid things. So I forgive you. However, what are you going to do about this?" Victoria went on.

"I am going to speak to Pastor James about this tomorrow. Hopefully, he will have some answers for me," Brittany said.

"I think that is a good idea. But I want you to take into consideration that this may not go the way you expect," Victoria cautioned.

"Yeah, I know," Brittany replied quietly.

"I am ready to face the consequences of my actions, too. I know Christopher will probably feel like I am throwing him under the bus, but it is not so much about him, rather, it is about me and what I have done, and the position I have put the ministry in and the impact it is having on the young people," Brittany said, sobbing in between phrases.

"I am really sorry that it took all of this for the scales to fall from your eyes but it is better later than never," Victoria stated.

"Will you pray with me, Vicky?" Brittany asked hesitantly.

"Of course!" Victoria stated. "We will pray together that the will of God be done in this situation."

Both girls started praying for each other and the situation that they were each facing. Victoria couldn't remember the last time that this had happened. She was grateful that God was restoring her relationship with her friend. In a world that was constantly about self, it was rare to have people that stick with you for the long haul. Most people walked away without trying to resolve their issues due to pride. They blame others for their losses without any accountability for themselves. In this moment, her heart overflowed with joy as she renewed her connection with her friend and with God.

Confession is good for the soul.

Unknown

CHAPTER 14

Brittany sat in Pastor James' office with her heart in her throat. She looked around nervously. She never really had a reason to come in here before. She had always kept out of trouble, too focused on ministry. So, she never really needed to speak to Pastor James about anything other than choir related matters - and that was usually minute, so it was done in a public setting. Yes, he was the youth pastor, and she reported to him, but they had always had an easy camaraderie.

Pastor James walked into the room with his easygoing swagger and megawatt smile. He reminded her of President Barack Obama. The confidence and bow-legged gait drew people's attention. She wondered sometimes why he chose to be a pastor. He could have easily been a male model. If truth be told, she found him to be quite easy on the eyes. He was at least six feet, four inches and even in her 6-inch heels, she never quite reached above his chest.

"Hello, Brittany, I am glad you could make it," he said in his bassy radio personality voice.

"Thanks for seeing me on such short notice, "Brittany returned.

"Of course," he responded.

She felt very small where he was concerned. He walked around to his side of the mahogany desk that glowed softly and settled into the broad, leather-back chair that seemed to shrink in size as he eased his body into it. Everything on his desk was meticulously arranged. As a matter of fact, his whole office was tidy, absolutely nothing out of place. She was comforted by that. She didn't understand why, but she was. She knew he had decorated it himself because he was a single man. In fact, every woman in the church knew that. And there were quite a few vying for his attention, but he politely told them all that he wasn't interested in pursuing a relationship with any of them. He was transparent and honest and the young people were enamored by him. He always kept his word to them. Whatever they told him in confidence was safe with him. She hoped she would receive the same treatment.

There was a knock on the door.

"Come in," Pastor James called, swiveling to face the door. Christopher walked into the office, shock registering on his face as he saw Brittany sitting there. When she had called to speak to Pastor James, she asked him to invite Chris, because she wanted to say what she had to in front of him. He thought that was big of her to do, and he had issued the invitation. She didn't know the specifics, but from the look on Christopher's face, he didn't know that she was going to be here.

Pastor James rose effortlessly and shook Christopher's hand across the desk, "Chris, I am glad that you could make it on such short notice. Please have a seat there." He gestured toward the seat across from Brittany.

"How are you today?" Pastor James asked politely.

"I am okay," Chris responded warily, his eyes darting to Brittany.

"Would anyone like a drink of water before we begin?" Pastor James asked.

"No, I am good. Thank you," Brittany said, making herself comfortable in her seat and folding her hands in her lap. She was a bit anxious, so she was trying to calm herself down.

"I will take some," Chris said, clearing his throat.

Pastor James walked across the carpeted office floor to a mini refrigerator tucked away in the corner, his feet making little to no noise. He returned with three bottles, even though Brittany had declined. He placed them on coasters in front of them, and returned to his seat.

"Before we begin, let's pray," he stated. He quickly bowed his head.

"Eternal and merciful father, we thank you for being God. We know that you are President and CEO of the universe and besides you there is no other that deserves all the praise and glory that we give unto you. We count it not robbery to celebrate you as our risen Lord, Savior and king. We place you on the highest throne of praise and exalt you because you are the only true wise and living God. We thank you God that you have kept us throughout the day and allowed us to meet together. Father, send your Holy Spirit to be a part of this meeting. Let your spirit comfort us and give us the right words to say. Let everything that we do be done in decency and order. Let your will be magnified at the end. Father, use me as your conduit to bless the lives of your people. Holy Spirit, please grant me wisdom, knowledge and understanding like you did unto Solomon to address any issues that may arise. Guide me to do it without partiality, favor or fear. Continue to speak through me and let your perfect will be done here tonight, in Jesus' name. Amen."

As Pastor James concluded, Brittany and Christopher echoed the sentiments and lifted their heads to face him.

"Okay. Let's get started," Pastor James stated, rubbing his hands together.

"All right, Brittany, you wanted to meet with Christopher and I, so tell us why that is," Pastor James said, leaning back in his chair, pressing his index fingers together and onto his lips.

Brittany straightened up in her chair and made eye contact with Pastor James. She heard Vicky's voice in her head.

"Speak up for yourself. Be honest and transparent, tell the truth, even if your voice shakes."

She did not look anywhere else as she let the story of Christopher's promiscuous behavior flow from her. After she had decided to talk with Pastor James, several other young ladies from the choir had come forward to her and confided in her, not knowing that she herself was a victim of Christopher. One of the girls, Latoya, found out she was pregnant a couple of months ago. Brittany effortlessly narrated Latoya's story, keeping her eyes fixed on Pastor James throughout.

When Latoya told Christopher the news, he had told her that he didn't want a child and that he would give her the money to get rid of the baby.

At this juncture of her narration, Brittany twisted her hands together. Out of the corner of her eye, she could see Christopher squirming in his chair, trying to get comfortable.

"...She couldn't tell anyone about it because she didn't know who to trust. She had told him she would think about it, but each day he kept calling and pressuring her to terminate the pregnancy," said Brittany undoubtedly, as if she was a witness.

Apparently, Christopher was not ready to be anyone's dad and Latoya knew she couldn't do it without him. She finally gave in and they went to a clinic on Flatbush Avenue and she had had an abortion. Christopher put her in a cab and sent her home. She didn't hear from him again. Each time she called him, it went to voicemail. She left umpteenth messages for him, but none were returned. When she tried to speak to him at church, he was always in conversation with someone else and said he couldn't speak with her. She finally came to the conclusion that she was no longer of any use to him. He had had his fill of her and had moved on to the next person. She was even more devastated when she realized he only wanted her for one thing and one thing only. So she stopped reaching out to him because she was tired of embarrassing herself. However, she was having a hard time with what she had done. Whenever she lay down, she kept feeling the cold metal object probing her inside. She couldn't sleep at night and everywhere she went she heard babies crying. She felt like she was losing her mind.

Plausibly, Latoya was sharing her predicament with Brittany in hopes that Brittany knew someone who could help her. Brittany had asked her if it was okay for her to disclose this to Pastor James, and she had given her consent. She was also willing to corroborate her story and provide evidence if that was needed.

As her voice shook and tears rolled down her face, Brittany continued her story. Instinctively, Pastor James leaned forward and extended the box of tissue to her. She grabbed a couple, apologized for her tears and blew her nose, bringing her story to a halt quite prematurely.

Pastor James assured her that it was okay and turned toward Christopher.

"Christopher, you hear the charges that are being made against you? Do you have anything to say?" Pastor James asked.

"They are all lying," Christopher answered quickly. "These women have quite the imagination, I can tell you that."

He then laughed condescendingly and shook his head.

"Pastor James, I don't know what they are talking about. They are trying to mar my reputation. These trifling women never like to see a good, black man prosper, always trying to bring him down with their lies," Christopher continued, his voice climbing.

Brittany saw Pastor James' shocked expression when Christopher used the word "trifling" to describe women. Christopher, however, didn't notice. He was too caught up in his rant to notice the body language of Pastor James.

"Even if Brittany is telling the truth, these women asked for it. You know how it is, Pastor James. These women walk around here pretending to be holy, pure and virtuous, while they are undercover freaks. They are like clothes pins - you squeeze their head with a little compliment and 'I love you' and they open their legs all too willingly for you. You hardly have to work for it," Christopher said. "I am sure you have had your fair share of sampling from them."

Brittany saw Pastor James' body stiffen and the vein in his right temple started to tick viciously. She saw his nostrils flare. Then, he clenched and unclenched his fists.

"I would mind how you speak to me and what you accuse me of, Christopher," he growled softly, causing the hairs on the back of her neck to stand at attention.

Unabashed, Christopher went on with his indictment.

"You want to tell me, with all these women who throw themselves at you, that you have not taken advantage of the situation?" he asked, widening his eyes and cocking his head to the side.

"These women here are no better than the women in the world. They pretend that they are but they are not. They walk around here behaving like they can't do any evil when all they do is evil. Church used to be a place where men, when they were ready to settle down, would go to find a wife. The women were chaste and virtuous, seeking God with their heart. Nowadays, these women are trying to be first lady to the pastor even though they know the pastor already legally has a first lady. They do it right under the first lady's nose, pretending to be her friend in the meanwhile. There is no respect or regard for the sanctity of marriage."

Brittany shook her head in horror as she listened to Chris spew his hateful jargon. He went on, refusing to watch his tone or his temper.

"For years I sat and watched as my beautiful, kind, spirit-filled mother put her best foot forward publicly for the sake of ministry. She smiled in public while her heart was broken by the most intense betrayal ever. She had to pray for, pray with, work with and help women, who were trying to demote her from the position of First Lady, just because they thought it was a glorified position to have. They looked at her clothing and the car she drove and not having a 9-5 job and deemed that is what they wanted, not seeing the sacrifices she made – the late nights she sat up praying for the church; the days she went without, so that some church members and or their kids could have something to eat; the times we were left to fend for ourselves because someone else needed her and she knew to say no would anger our father; the times she heard them with her own ears diminishing her worth and character as not being good enough for the "Man of God" and kept right on giving her all.

Christopher was a burning inferno and continued on in hot passion.

"These women here are no different. They gossip about each other, and dress to impress in the latest fashions that they can't afford, all to astound people who don't really care about them. They have no substance, all flash - just hair well done and face full of makeup. They are all white-washed sepulchers, willing to do anything for a little bit of attention. Add the word marriage to the equation and you have them hooked, eager to do anything to please you for some time, attention and a promise ring. I just help them out," Christopher laughed mockingly. "As a man you know how it is."

Christopher looked Pastor James square in the eyes for his approval as if to say, "tell me I'm lying."

"We men see how many notches we can put on our beds and belt before we marry that ordinary one we keep at home while we continue doing our thing with the woman/women on the side," Christopher stated bluntly, sitting back and resting his right ankle on his left thigh.

Brittany sat through his diatribe in shock. The man speaking was someone she didn't know. She couldn't believe the words that were coming out of Christopher's mouth.

'*Who is this person?* she thought to herself. She could not believe she had been so gullible.

"You and I are nothing alike," Pastor James said, rising. "You were placed in a leadership role within this church because you presented yourself to be an upright young man whose passion was for God and the things of God. You are supposed to be a Christian, which means like Christ, an example to your peers and others around you. And this is how you abuse your position in the church? To exploit the affection of these young women, who thought you were godly and thought you meant to do right by them? You knew full well that you had no desire to do so. That is the worst deceit possible," Pastor James stated, leaning over the desk at Christopher.

"You are taking this heifer's word over mine?" Christopher countered angrily back at Pastor James. "I didn't do anything they didn't want, begged or asked me to do."

Christopher rose hotly to his feet.

Before he could finish his sentence, Pastor James was standing in front of Christopher.

He leaned his face into Christopher's.

"This is my office and you will have respect here. I would watch my next words wisely if I were you," he growled through his teeth.

Christopher remained silent.

"I am very sorry for what you have experienced as a child and the things that your mother had to go through. You need to get help because you are bleeding on people who've never done anything except love you. I'll recommend someone for you to see if you would like," Pastor James said, trying to remain composed.

Christopher shook his head in the negative.

"However, as of tonight, you will no longer be employed by this church. I can't stop you from worshipping here, but you will never play here again without a major change in your life. You have a form of godliness, but you have no relationship with God. I will inform the Bishop and the church board of what happened here tonight. We will get the young ladies that you have damaged the necessary treatment to put them back on the right path, but Christopher, I can assure you, that if I hear about you and any of these young ladies in this church, you will have me to reckon with. Do you understand me?"

"Yes, sir. I do," Christopher answered, his voice trembling.

"Please leave my office," Pastor Joseph stated calmly but forcefully.

Christopher hustled from the room, without a backward glance.

Brittany sat there in amazement at what just transpired. She knew it would be a difficult situation but this was beyond her wildest imagination. Things had escalated rather quickly, but she was thankful that it was all over. The weight of the world was finally lifted from her shoulders.

She lifted her head to see Pastor James, looking at her. He was only five years older than her, but on nights like tonight, he exuded a measure of wisdom and maturity that made him seem so much older and mature.

"Brittany, I am proud of the strength that you portrayed here tonight. I know it could not have been easy," Pastor James said, moving back to sit in his seat.

"I am happy that you were able to come forth not only for yourself but for the others that were suffering because of Christopher. That was a great thing that you did. However, I am going to request that you take a three-month sabbatical from leading the choir. You are brilliant at what you do, and no one does it like you, but when your gift, flesh and self take precedence over your relationship with God, that is a slippery slope that you are on...and you saw where it took you. You did not hear the Spirit telling you that conducting a sexual affair while being a minister in the house of God was wrong. God will never take his gifts and talents from you but his anointing will leave because He cannot operate in unclean temples. You have been offering strange fire unto God and because He is patient and kind with us, you and Christopher are not consumed. What we do here is too important to the kingdom of God for us to allow anyone to jeopardize it. You are an amazing young woman, beautiful, intelligent and deserve the world, but you have allowed your flesh and the desires of the world to blind you from the things that are more important and lasting. I hope that during this sabbatical you will find the strength and courage to have a real true relationship with God that will not be shaken so easily by the desires of the flesh," Pastor James finished.

Brittany bowed her head in shame and her shoulder sank.

"Britt…I mean, Brittany, there is nothing to be ashamed of," Pastor James said, coming around the desk.

He knelt before her.

"Please lift your head and walk in the fear of God. It was just a mistake… everyone makes them. It does not mean that you are not a good person. However, if you continue to make them you are going to lose your way," he said, looking into her soul with his piercing gaze.

"Let me pray with you before you leave, if that is okay with you?" he offered.

"Yes, it is," Brittany said, grabbing his hands for dear life.

She couldn't help thinking that his hands were very soft for a man; however, the thought vanished when he started praying for her. At that moment, she realized that this is what she needed, a man who would cover her and seek God for her the way Pastor James was doing. Never once, while she was with Christopher, did they ever pray together. She didn't even know if he could pray. In that moment, Brittany vowed to seek the will and way of God with her whole heart and not be distracted anymore. She would wait for her Boaz like Victoria was doing. She would wait. No matter how long it took, she would be a wife in waiting.

Be not deceived; God is not mocked: for whatsoever

a man soweth, that shall he also reap.

Galatians 6:7

CHAPTER 15

Christopher was pissed! He stormed out of the auditorium cursing under his breath. He punched the door open, ignoring the pain in his hand. He was so angry that he felt his body growing warm as his temper rose. How dare Pastor James take that heifer Brittany's word over his?! Brittany was going to get what was coming to her. He would make sure of it. She had made him lose his job and someone needed to pay for that.

He stormed toward the parking lot where his car sat. He got in and started pounding the steering wheel. Christopher started screaming like a mad man. The expletives that rained from his lips would have made the most seasoned sailor blush. He started his car and sped out of the lot leaving gravel in his wake. He turned left on to the main street and sped down the block. He halted abruptly in the middle of the street when he almost ran into a steel garbage pail lying in his path. Could this night get any worse?

Christopher jumped out of his car, cursing, and went around to the front of the car to move the garbage pail. The headlights blinded him to the guys stepping out from the sidewalk. He jumped when he heard voices.

"Hey, you need some help?" one of the guys asked.

"Nah, man. I'm good," Christopher said.

"You sure, dude?" another one asked.

"Yeah, man. I'm cool," Christopher replied, trying to locate them in the dark. How many of them were there? He wasn't certain. He didn't notice anyone when he was coming down the street, but then again he wasn't paying much attention to what was happening around him.

"By the way, is your name Christopher Martin?" the first guy asked.

"Yeah! Who's asking?" Christopher queried with a false sense of bravado. He realized that he was surrounded by at least four of them. One of them was even sitting on the hood of his car.

"Dude, get up off my car," Christopher said.

"Oh my bad," the guy said, getting up and placing his hand on his chest.

As he unfurled himself, Christopher realized his mistake. The guy was at least six feet, six inches and towered over Christopher. The anger Christopher was feeling dissipated and was replaced by a sense of foreboding. His palms began to sweat and his mouth became dry. The guy bent back over the car and used the right sleeve of his shirt to rub at the spot where he was sitting.

"There you go," he said. "—All better." He let out a smile. But somehow, the smile never really reached his eyes.

"It's cool, man. No worries," Christopher said, tossing the garbage pail that he was holding and moving toward the open door of his car. Suddenly his world became dark as a bag was placed over his head. He cried out in pain as his arms were grabbed and quickly yanked and tied behind his back. Christopher struggled and kicked against his assailants but he was overpowered and could hardly move.

He was pushed into the back seat of his own car, and he started screaming. Someone punched him in the stomach and demanded he shut up. Chris kept on screaming. The salty taste of his blood filled his mouth as he was smack repeatedly in the face by a hard metal object. He stopped screaming instantaneously, but the tears continued to flow. He tried to hear what the guys were saying, but his heart was pounding too loudly in his ear, making everything inaudible. Christopher had never felt more afraid in his life. He began to pray and beg God for his life. He tried bargaining. He promised that if God spared his life he would turn over a new page – be a changed man, and do right by Him. He didn't want to die.

He could feel sweat in torrents making a mad dash down his face, neck and back. His shirt clung to him as a second skin.

"Yo! We are almost there," the driver yelled over the music blaring from the stereo. *Almost where?* Christopher thought. Fear wrapped his gaunt hand around his heart and he lost control of his bowels.

"What is that smell?" the guy on the right side of him asked. The guy flew up out of the seat when he realized what was happening.

"Dude, pull the car over!" the guy on the left side of the car yelled angrily.

"This negro done messed himself," he said, hissing his teeth.

The other guy on his left side started cursing and punching him in his face and neck. Christopher moaned in pain but tried not to make too much noise. He didn't want to make them any angrier than they already were. The driver and the guy in the front passenger seat started laughing.

"Yo, hold on. We'll be there in one minute," the driver said.

"Roll down the window, man," said the guy sitting on his left side. "I can't believe this punk did that. That is going to be one mess for someone to clean."

They laughed even harder and Christopher felt shame take over him. The car began to slow and Christopher felt the unevenness of the road he was on. He knew whatever was going to happen to him was going to happen here. He felt a fresh flood of fear take hold of him and he began to shake, whimper and cry. The car came to a complete stop and the driver said, "Get him out."

Christopher was dragged from the car and tossed to the ground.

"Pick him up," said someone to the left of him.

He was dragged unceremoniously to his feet. The bag that covered his head was ripped off. Christopher blinked furiously, trying to see, adjusting his eyes to the light. Stars danced behind his lids and it took a while for him to focus. As his eyes cleared, he saw that he was surrounded by four big dudes — the type you saw at the gym with the veins popping out of their tree trunk arms and legs. He could hear the chirping of crickets which meant they were in some place on the outskirts of town, a place where if he screamed no one would hear him. Christopher was terrified.

"What do you want from me?" he stammered.

"How about your life?" one of the guys responded.

Christopher turned to look at him. He was the smallest of the guys but he had the meanest face.

"Why would you want my life? What did I do to you? I don't even know who you are!" Christopher started crying.

"You don't need to know us. The fact is we know you and we know what type of dude you are. You messed with the wrong dude's sister, making promises you never meant to keep, just so that you could get into her panties. Someone needs to teach you a lesson."

He got up into Christopher's face and yelled angrily. Christopher felt his face being covered in spittle but dared not move.

"Untie his hands and let him go," he said to the other guys.

They did as he commanded them. Christopher rubbed his wrist, trying to return blood flow to his fingers. He was blinded by a blow to the left side of his face. Christopher felt his lips split and pain ricocheted through his head. Before he could comprehend what was happening he was given an uppercut that caused his head to snap back. Christopher fell backward on the ground. He felt a boot hit his rib and he was certain he heard his ribs snap. The pain made him gasp for breath. He curled himself up in a fetal position and tried to hide his face from the boot that came relentlessly at him. He felt blood pouring into his eye from the gash that opened up when the guy stomped his head into the ground. His face was on fire and his ear kept ringing. One thing he was grateful for was that it was the only one guy pummeling him into the earth. The others just stood by and watched as their friend rained a hellish beating on Christopher. The rest of the gang said absolutely nothing.

"Please God, don't let them kill me," he begged silently. But there was no response from God.

To Christopher, the assault on his person continued for what seemed like hours. But in actuality, it was only five minutes.

"That is enough!" said the guy that sat on the hood of Christopher's car.

"I think he gets the idea," he said while squatting in front of Christopher.

"Look at me," he said softly to Christopher.

Christopher tried to focus through the one eye that remained slightly open.

"I know where you live," he said, showing Christopher his driver's license.

He didn't know when they had taken it from him.

"Don't go getting any smart ideas about identifying us," he said softly.

Christopher ached through silent sobs as his attacker spoke.

"I heard a saying a while ago from Bob Marley that I am going to share with you. Bro Bob said, the biggest coward is a man who awakens a woman's love without the intention of loving her. You, my friend, are a punk who uses the affection of a woman for your own gain," he said.

He continued eerily and softly as if he wanted to burn the words into Christopher's brain.

"I want you to remember something. Not every woman out here is loose and without morals. Not every woman out here doesn't have brothers or men to defend her honor when leeches like you try to take advantage of them. Not every woman out here is ashamed to call you out on your lies, pretension and manipulation of her feelings and to hold you accountable for falling short when your lies are being highlighted. A few of them have brothers, uncles, nephews and sons who will give you the beat down that these women can't. Just because they are weaker in size, you think they have to take your bullcrap. Well, we are your size and we can handle you."

The guy continued, his voice becoming louder with his anger.

"I will be keeping an eye on you Christopher," he said, tapping the license in his palm. "And if I hear or see anything, I will be back, I promise you."

He rose to his full height and walked away.

Two of the other guys flanked Christopher and held him down. The third one came and held Christopher's face. He flicked open the blade. At the sight of the blade reflecting in the light, Christopher began to scream. The guy placed his elephant size hand over Christopher's mouth. Christopher struggled, twisting back and forth trying to get out the path of the blade but he couldn't move. As the blade made contact with his skin, Christopher let out muted screams.

More blood ran down his face as the sharp blade razor danced joyfully in a zig-zagged fashion, opening his skin as it skipped from his ear to his mouth. Christopher lost consciousness.

He did not see when the cherry red BMW pulled up next to his car and the petite young lady got out so that her brother could get behind the wheel. He did not feel it when she walked over to him and kicked him twice in his abdomen with her Louboutin-shrouded foot.

"That's for my baby," she said and spat on him.

She turned and walked back to the car. One of the guys held the door open for her to get in, before walking to the front passenger seat and getting in himself. Latoya sat back in the seat and folded her expertly manicured hands across her chest. She never took her eyes off Christopher's battered and bloodied body until she could no longer see him. It was the first time she felt better in months. She met her brother's eye in the mirror and smiled. It was the first time he had seen her do so in months. He smiled in return and turned his attention back to the road.

There are always going to be things you look back on

and wish you did differently but those very choices

made you exactly who you are today.

Unknown

CHAPTER 16

Victoria looked up at the ceiling, trying to figure out how she was going to tell Richard she couldn't marry him. She thought she had the perfect opportunity two months ago when they went out to dine. Finally, they were getting the opportunity to really talk without anyone around and she had promised herself that she would let him know how she felt. As she opened her mouth to address the issue, Richard exclaimed.

"Look who is here!"

She turned to look in the direction that held Richard's rapt attention. Her heart did a half vault somersault and flopped into her stomach. Her palms began to sweat and her tongue became dry and heavy. She lost all coherent thoughts and simply stared.

Entering the room was Nick. His mother had christened him Nicholas Parker but everyone called him Nick. He looked as scrumptious as usual. As he came further into the room with that confident swagger of his, he looked like he had just stepped out the pages of GQ. The fact that he looked so good wasn't helping her already rapid pulse rate. Nick rarely dressed up. He was more of a jeans and T-shirt with boots kind of guy but when he chose to garb up, he could stop traffic as he was doing now. Victoria was sure that she was not the only one staring at him. She looked around and she was right. All the other women were either blatantly staring or taking sly glimpses at him so that the men they were with would not be upset. He always had that effect when he stepped into a room; he had a magnetism that drew women to him no matter what he was wearing or where he was headed. When she first started dating him (what seemed to be like eons ago), she would have a conniption every time they went out and women gawked at him. However, over time, she had learned to let it go and let it be. Nick was going to be Nick. He was a very friendly guy and quite sociable –"too friendly" used to be her thought. But every time she said that to him, it only cracked him up and caused him to tease her mercilessly about her being jealous and not wanting to share him with the world. Therefore, she just took it in stride.

"Nick, over here!" she heard Richard yell.

What in the hell was going on here? she queried quietly to herself. She didn't know that Richard knew Nick.

"Oh Lord, please come now," she pleaded under her breath and then tried to sink into her chair and through the floor. However, gravity was not having any of that and she remained where she was. Her heart started thumping in her chest and she swore the entire room could hear it. She tried to appear nonchalant as Nick approached by taking a sip of her water. But her hand was shaking so badly she had to place the glass back down before she made a fool of herself by spilling the water everywhere.

"Hi Richard," she heard Nick say.

Richard stood up to hug him and immediately she compared them. She knew it was wrong to do so but she could not help herself. They were about the same height.

I guess I like my men tall, she thought sarcastically.

With the exception of them both being unquestionably handsome, that was where the likeness ended. They both filled out their suits, but Richard had a tendency to be soft around the middle. That was not the case with Nick. Personal experience had taught her that the body encased in that black suit was nothing but sheer muscle. Victoria knew what was under that suit because he had stripped down so many times at the beach and pool and had played touch football bareback in the park with their friends during the summer barbecues. In addition, she spent many of her winter days with her arms wrapped around that middle as they cuddled and talked. Where she was always cold, Nick was the extreme opposite. He was a living breathing furnace, always hot, so in the winter months she was always snuggled close to him for warmth.

Victoria tried to catch her breath from that thought.

Behave! she said to herself.

It wasn't as if they had slept together - not for lack of trying on Nick's part. She never quite understood men's obsession with sex. Yes, it was quite the pleasurable event - and it could be a very beautiful thing, when done right with the right person. Yet, most men she knew seemed to have a fixation on it. She had cornered her co-worker and church sister - Rita's husband Josh - one Sunday evening while they were hanging in the living room after dinner, and asked him, why this was. With much reluctance, after immense coaxing and Rita's prompting, Josh finally acquiesced.

Josh, sitting on the arm of the tan loveseat where Rita sat said, "Men are visual creatures. We are moved by what we see."

He went on to say that he remembered exactly what Rita was wearing the day he met her and began to recount the tale.

One Sunday, he was driving down Utica Avenue and stopped at a red light on Utica and Avenue D. She was crossing the street. She had a pixie haircut that highlighted her bone structure. She was wearing a fitted, silky, floral dress that conformed to her body, and moved with her when she moved. It hit her mid-calf and she was wearing beige stiletto heels. Despite the unevenness of the street, she walked like she was wearing flats. She didn't hurry, but walked purposefully. Someone coming from the opposite direction beckoned to her and she turned to smile at them as they walked past.

"I thought she was looking at me and smiling," said Josh. "My heart immediately started to thump furiously, like it wanted to jump out of my chest and I had this sudden desire to speak with her."

Josh looked down at his wife.

"You never told me any of this," Rita said blushing.

"I didn't want to let you know that you had my heart from that moment we met," Richard said cheekily. He bent over and kissed his wife.

Victoria felt slightly embarrassed as she watched them kiss for a very long time. For a minute, Victoria thought they had forgotten about her. She cleared her throat, and Rita jumped out of her skin. She opened glazed eyes to look at Vicky and blushed some more. They *had* forgotten about her. Victoria laughed out loud as Josh said, "I still have it."

Rita became a beet in the face.

"Anyways, let me finish this story," Josh continued.

"I pulled over to the side of the road, got out to talk with her, only to see her getting on the bus," he said.

"That was the week my car was in the shop," said Rita. "Someone had run a red light and ran into me and all for the grace of God I am still here. So I took it to the shop that week. However, that Sunday I didn't want to miss church so I took a cab there and decided to take the scenic route back to my home."

She stroked Josh's hand.

"I knew I had to talk to her, so I jumped in my car and followed the bus for half an hour, looking for the stop where she would get off. When she finally did, I went up to speak to her. That was the beginning of my life," Josh said, looking at Rita in her eyes.

Victoria realized that she needed to leave soon because they were creating some moments here that she didn't want to intrude on.

"I said all that to say," continued Josh. "...That men are visual creatures. And for a man, if the woman looks good, it will cause him to be aroused and his body will want to quench that thirst, regardless of whether or not he is in a relationship, married, engaged or whatever. His major concern is the satisfaction of his body. So, sleeping with a woman, one that he doesn't love, is no issue for a man. Once he gets his pleasure, he doesn't have to have his emotions involved. Most men compartmentalize when it comes to sex and love. Both don't have to go hand in hand."

Josh chose his next few words carefully.

"Women, on the other hand, well... most women... have their emotions tied to giving their bodies to their men. It is a woman's way of expressing how she feels without actually verbalizing what she is feeling. Her body is her most prized possession and for her to give it to him, it testifies of how much she cares for him, or is caring for him," Josh concluded.

Victoria sat bug-eyed listening to Josh unfold the "mystery" of why men slept around. She and Rita laughed heartily as he hurriedly removed his meal from the microwave and left stating he would not be discussing this any further.

After that talk, Josh avoided her, saying she asked too many questions and if the male species knew that he had told her what he did, they would evict him from the men's club like they did with Steve Harvey after he wrote *Act like A lady, Think like A Man*. He did not want anything to do with her information-gathering jaunt and told her not to ask him anymore questions about it.

Victoria shook her head to dislodge the memory and returned to what was happening in front of her.

"Meet my fiancée, Vicky," Richard announced.

She saw the shock register in Nicholas' eyes but he quickly masked it. Things had not ended amicably for them and they hadn't seen or spoken to each other for about 18 months now — she had made sure of that. But she was positive that the last person Nick expected to see was her and the last thing he expected to hear was that she was engaged so soon after they parted ways.

"Nice to meet you," Nick said.

"Likewise," she answered.

He had stretched out his hand for her to shake it. She didn't want to, but it would be awkward if she didn't. She touched his hand slightly and tried to quickly pull away. Nick, however, was not having that as he clasped her hand tightly and held it while he asked when the wedding would be.

"Next two months," chimed Richard.

Vicky winced as Nick's clasp tightened, causing the ring on her right hand, the one that Nick had given her for her birthday — the princess-cut, diamond-encrusted ten carat, platinum promise ring — to bite into her flesh. He stared at her and then slowly released his grip.

"This is Nicole," Nick said.

It was then that Vicky caught sight of the wallflower.

Stop it Victoria! What did you expect him to do? To stop breathing because you guys were no longer together? She chastised herself.

Victoria critiqued Nicole. She really wasn't a wallflower by any degree. Of course, most men would say she was pretty; it was just that she was not anything to brag about either as far as Victoria was concerned. Nicole was a petite, dark-skinned girl with a heart-shaped face. On closer inspection, Victoria saw that she was struggling with an acne problem and silently smirked. She was dressed in a black top with skin-tight spandex pants that left little to the imagination. She had what Victoria's brothers would call a 'waiter-booty' – meaning her butt was big enough to rest a glass on without worrying. Her breasts were by no means huge but still seemed as if they could pop out of the top she was wearing at the next breath she took.

"Hi!" Nicole said instantly.

Vicky noted that she had a squeaky voice.

Two things I am not liking here, said the demon on Vicky's left shoulder.

She is a sweet girl with a beautiful smile, said the angel on the right, drawing Vicky's attention back to Nicole who was smiling at Richard.

She does have a nice smile and good teeth, Vicky reluctantly admitted but she was tending to lean more to the side of the demon than the angel. She did not like Nicole, not one bit. She knew why she was feeling like that but she would not admit it to anyone but herself. She had heard about Nicole from mutual friends she once shared with Nick. She never placed any weight on it because Nick was never serious about anyone for too long - well, maybe with the exception of her, but look at where that had gotten her even with them dating on and off for five years! So, that really didn't count either. But then Nicole seemed to have what it took to keep his attention after all, if he was bringing her to this fancy restaurant in the city.

"Join us," she heard Richard say.

Like hell they are, she said to herself.

"I am sure they have other plans and want to be alone," Victoria said aloud, shooting daggers at Richard with her eyes.

"As a matter of fact we don't," said Nick, smiling - a smile that never reached his grey eyes.

"Then it's settled. Waiter, bring us two more chairs," Richard bellowed, scooting closer to Victoria to make room for Nick and his wallflower.

Victoria was a lady in every sense of the word. She didn't fuss or fight over a man. She knew her worth. But love does strange things to a person; it makes one lose one's pride just to please the one that has your heart. She knew about that firsthand. Many times while in the relationship with Nick, she would be the one to apologize first, to ensure the peace and the continuity of the relationship. She had even forgotten the hurts that were done to her by the people who said they loved her. She would have done anything for Nick. She had forsaken friends for Nick, and she had even diminished her relationship with God for Nick. He was her all until that fateful night 18 months ago...

The creaking of the dressing room door brought her back to the present.

Victoria looked up and froze.

There is time for everything, and a season for

every activity under the heavens:

Ecclesiastes 3:1

CHAPTER 17

Nick sat in the church in a state of disbelief. Not for one moment in his life would he have believed that this would be the reality of his situation. He had come to the wedding to prove to himself that it was really happening. When Richard had issued the invitation a month ago, he accepted. If this was a prank, it sure was quite an elaborate one and it wasn't funny anymore. He couldn't believe that "his" Vicky was getting married. He still thought of her as his. No other woman had meant as much to him as Victoria had and still did. He had had his share of women from the time he started sprouting chest hairs until now. With his height and mixed racial heritage of black and white, he knew he was handsome, more handsome than the normal "black brother."

He had known this from the time he was five years old. But it came home to him when he started high school. Girls were always asking him out and wanting to be with him. He had gotten one of the girls everyone wanted. Her name was Tatyana; she was a year younger than him and was fine! Brothers would have done anything just to be associated with her, but she never paid them any mind. She acted like she was too good to be seen with them. When it came to him, though, she always smiled and was nice to him. One day in chemistry class, she passed him a note with her number on it. It wasn't long before they were making out after school, cutting class and going to her house. Two months later, he introduced her to sex. He loved her. She was special to him. He had made it plain to the other girls that he was no longer available. He was faithful to her and did all in his power to ensure that she was happy. They hung out together every chance they got. They were inseparable. Until one day he walked in on her kissing another guy at one of their friend's house parties. He stood there looking at her, rage building in his chest, and clenching and unclenching his fist. She gasped when she saw him. She started to apologize, but he never heard it. He walked out on her that day, promising himself that a woman would never make him feel like that again. He resorted to playing the games men and women played and he never looked back.

He was what his sister Sarai would call the Mac Daddy of the game. He played but he was always careful to never to be too emotionally invested in any one woman. That is why he was always talking to at least three women at any given time and constantly had them in rotation. They never knew about each other. He always made a woman feel like she was the only one in his life and the only one for him. He had broken quite a few hearts along the way. He always kept them as friends, though; there was no reason to burn the bridge if you didn't have to. He never knew when he would be up late and need a warm body. In addition, they were always willing to give him a second chance, thinking that he had changed. Sometimes he wondered how women could still be so gullible even after being hurt repeatedly by the same individual.

The pastor making his way to Richard at the front reminded Nicholas of the first time he had seen Victoria. It was in a church setting, but for a much more somber event - a funeral. Victoria was walking past when someone bumped her right into his side. He will forever swear that when she collided with him he felt like he was being electrocuted. Her pocketbook had fallen, spilling all the contents onto the floor. She bent swiftly to retrieve her stuff and he felt compelled to help. She thanked him and smiled at him. That smile was his undoing. His heart felt like someone had pressed pause on it then hit fast forward immediately after. The smile transformed her face and lit up her eyes. Was it his imagination or did her eyes change color? She walked away without a backward glance, which was strange. Most women didn't do that to him; they always took a second look at him and wanted to know more about him. Nick decided that he wanted to know who she was. For the remainder of the night, he kept asking everyone who she was. Finally, he struck gold in the form of his sister Sarai. She knew Victoria really well. They had gone to college together and were best friends. He wondered how he never met her before, then again he was hardly ever home. He learned from his sister that Victoria had signed up for a cooking class. He enrolled himself in that very class. He would see Victoria, or Vicky as Sarai called her, and at the same time learn how to do more than boil water. It was a win-win situation.

The first day of class was great. Victoria remembered him and they paired up to do class work. After that, he just took it from there. He put his Mac Daddy experience to work and soon they were inseparable. He liked being with Victoria; she was brilliant, and challenged him on levels that not many women he had known were able to. She was funny in a sarcastic way, beautiful, friendly, outgoing, spontaneous, adventurous and confident. But she was also a little bit crazy, which he liked even more. Victoria kept him on his toes. She was not blinded as the other ladies were to the side women he had. She recognized the game and called him out on it many times. But he just played it off by telling her that she was jealous. That usually ended the conversation because she was too proud and independent for anyone to label her as jealous. But he saw how she watched him.

He was spending a lot more time with her but he still had the rotation going. He was not "macking" as hard but he couldn't see himself with one woman at that time. Few people knew about her, yet he didn't mind when his friends linked him to her. Victoria was someone he would be proud to be seen with. Over the years, they had broken up and gotten back together several times. Usually, it was his fault. It seemed like Vicky had some radar when he was up to no good because she always found out when he was up to his old tricks. She would get pissed and not talk to him, while he begged and apologized.

She would give him the cold shoulder for weeks and then forgive him, then things would go right back the way they were before, as if they had never been separated or stopped speaking to each other.

Nicholas knew she loved him very much; she made no qualms about telling him even if he did not respond in kind. She was confident in herself and her love for him. She was never afraid to show him how much she felt for him in whatever she did. He could not believe that she was sticking with him after all the things he had put her through. Soon, he began to get tired of his little black book. When he was with other women, all he could think about was Vicky and what she was doing. He was reforming and had cut down on the other girls he talked to. It had come down to just Vicky and one other girl, but he knew whom he would choose if push came to shove. But that was not a choice he would get to make. Before he could decide, his life began to spiral out of his control.

Memories don't leave like people do.

Tom Jones

CHAPTER 18

The bridal party started coming down the aisle and Nick grimaced.

This is a nightmare, he thought. Why didn't I just tell her how I felt? Idiot! He reprimanded himself internally.

Vicky and he had been in a really good place. She was spending a lot more time with him, even blowing off her friends to chill when he would call spontaneously. No matter the time of night, if he called or texted her, he would get a response. He smiled as he thought of one night when he had called her. He was sitting outside her apartment in the car and he felt like messing with her. It was only 11:30 pm but he knew she would be asleep. He never worried about her seeing someone else or putting a game on him; what you saw with her is what you got. She was an open book plus Vicky liked sleeping and, if she didn't have anything to do, you could find her either curled up with a good book in bed or actually just sleeping. That girl could sleep. It was after the third ring that he heard her groggy hello.

"Are you sleeping?" he had asked.

"Not anymore," she responded smartly and he smiled.

She could be mean if you woke her and she was definitely not a morning person, but he loved messing with her at those times. Even in the midst of her sleep she was a force to be reckoned with. Her brain seemed to be always on speed dial for a tongue-in-cheek retort.

"What are you doing?" he questioned.

"Umm…I was sleeping until somebody decided to ruin my beautiful dream," she retorted, yet he could hear the smile in her voice.

No matter what, she always made him feel like he was welcome in her world and that he belonged.

"Open the door," he said as he walked up to the entrance of the apartment. He heard the buzzer and knew that she had made her way through the apartment without turning the lights on even half-asleep. She was freakily intuitive like that.

When he got to her apartment, the door stood open, but Vicky was nowhere to be seen. He smiled. He knew where she would be and he was correct. As his eyes grew accustomed to the darkness, he saw her curled up on the queen-size bed. He knew she'd be wearing her Betty Boop peejays and headscarf. It was her die-hard uniform. She had those things in every color and texture imaginable. The confidence she exuded made her beautiful whether dressed in a two-piece business suit or with her headscarf and no makeup. She scooted over to the other half of the bed, inviting him in. He took off his shoes and climbed in.

"Imma have to give you your own keys. This waking-me-up business is not going to work," she mumbled groggily.

He chuckled. She always complained about him waking her, but then he knew she did not mind.

"I missed you," she said and wrapped her arms around his middle. Her fingers stroked his tummy for a bit, branding him wherever she touched, then they became still. He kissed her on the frontal lobe and nestled her tightly to his side. She fit perfectly, and he breathed in her clean scent. She always smelled like honeysuckles with a hint of jasmine.

He slowly dragged his finger along her arm. Her skin was silky soft like that of a baby. He had never felt skin like this on a woman before and his fingers always craved the touch. Before he had gotten here, he was agitated by some events that were taking place at his firm. Now a peace came over him and he closed his eyes, knowing that soon he would be fast asleep. It always happened like this, no matter what was going on with him, as soon as he was with Vicky, nothing seemed so bad or difficult that he could not handle. She was his home away from home. He knew that she was quickly becoming an integral part of his life. She was the first person he thought of in the mornings and the last person he thought of at night. It didn't matter where they were once Vicky was there it felt like home. She was his world and his love. He felt like a giddy teenager when he thought about her.

"I love you," he whispered against her head.

Victoria did not hear the one thing she craved more than the air she breathed. With her head on his chest, she had already taken the train back to la la land, lured by the heartbeat of the man that she loved more than life itself.

To trust God in the light is nothing, but to trust

Him in the dark – that is faith.

C.H. Spurgeon

CHAPTER 19

Victoria's heart fluttered wildly in her chest as though trying to escape. Tears filled her eyes and raced down her cheeks. She couldn't believe what she was seeing. She had made some prayer requests but she didn't expect them to be answered in this fashion. Yet, here's the proof that God still answers prayer and the reminder that you have to be careful with what you ask for.

"You need to stop being so dramatic," Helen admonished laughingly, bending to retrieve the bouquet laying on the floor. She rose gracefully and smiled broadly at her stupefied friend.

Victoria remained frozen in place, not daring to believe what she thought was impossible. Helen placed the bouquet on the lone table and turned to Victoria.

"Cat got your tongue? Don't I get a hug?" she asked.

"Of course you do!" Victoria exclaimed, rushing to give Helen a hug. She embraced her friend closely and sobbed with joy at the beautiful unexpected gift. She didn't realize how much she missed Helen's presence until now.

After a few minutes of shared hugs and Helen trying to soothe her tears, Victoria stepped back and stood, staring at Helen.

"I am real, Vicky," Helen said, laughing. "Don't be like doubting Thomas."

"I just can't believe that you are here," Victoria exclaimed.

"How? When? Where are you staying? Why didn't you tell me that you were coming?"

"I wanted it to be a surprise and, from the looks of things, I think I succeeded outstandingly," Vicky chortled.

"You know I don't like surprises."

"I'm aware, but as Ecclesiastes says, there is a time and season for everything under the sun and this, my darling, was the right time and season for this."

Helen touched Vicky's face lovingly and softly.

The floodgates opened once more, and Victoria held her head back trying not to do more damage to her makeup. It was a good thing she had chosen to wear her Maybelline waterproof mascara. She didn't want to think what she would look like if she hadn't.

"Thank you," she said, giving Helen another hug. "This is the best gift anyone could have given me today. I love and appreciate you so much for this. You don't know what this means to me."

She didn't realize how much she had missed Helen's calm presence in the midst of the chaos she has been facing in her life.

"Let's fix that makeup. I don't want to be the one responsible for you not looking your fabulous self on today of all days. Let me get that makeup artist back in here," Helen stated, turning toward the door.

"No, not yet. They can wait a few more minutes."

Victoria grabbed Helen's hand and walked to the only couch in the room.

"You look so beautiful," Victoria commented en route.

"This old thing?" Helen queried, pausing to look down at herself questioningly and shrugged. "Stop flattering me."

"No, you are absolutely gorgeous! You are working that dress, honey! " Victoria raved, standing next to her.

The woman looking back at Victoria was such a stark contrast from the one she had met over a year ago. Helen stood across from her - glowing. Her chocolate skin with its bronze sun-kissed tan shone beautifully. Helen was dressed in a strapless beige and gold mermaid sequin dress. It hugged the curves of her body. She was no longer brutishly thin as she was a year ago. She had these womanish curves in all the right places and the dress complemented each one as it flowed to the floor. She wore gold shoes that played peekaboo from beneath the dress whenever she moved. Her once curly hair was now straightened, parted down the middle, and pulled back tightly in a ponytail at the base of her head. She wore gold teardrop earrings and her face was flawlessly made up to highlight her high cheekbones and full lips. She was a beautiful woman to behold.

"You are certainly good for my ego, Vicky," Helen laughed delightfully.

Victoria finished her dart to the couch. She dragged Helen down with her and held on to her hand. The sense of déjà vu pervaded Victoria's senses as she looked across at Helen.

She wore an air of calm and peace that immediately started soothing Victoria's frazzled nerves. Time in the Caribbean seemed to have done more prodigiously for her than just offering her that sun-kissed glow.

"How have you been?! Tell me everything!" Victoria pleaded.

Helen's silvery laughter reverberated throughout the room. Her entire body shook as she laughed.

"I am beginning to think I should have waited until after the ceremony to make my presence known," Helen chided lovingly.

"No! This is what I needed. God knew that I needed you here and now to get through this, so you are right on time," Victoria admitted.

"Really? Is everything okay?"

"It really isn't, but it is too late to do anything about it right now."

"What?! It is never too late, Vicky. You know that. You convinced me of that, remember?" she told Victoria, squeezing her hand tightly and looking piercingly into her eyes. "What do you need me to do to help?"

"How about we stop talking about me for a minute and you answer my question?" Victoria emphasized.

"Touché! Savage!" Helen said, laughing.

"I am great, Victoria. The best I have ever been in a while. When I left you last year, I didn't know what to expect when I got on that plane. On the ride home, my mind was racing. What would I tell my parents? How would they react to my presence without the degree they sent me to pursue? I kept praying and asking God for the right words to say and for favor with them. I was nervous. I wanted my parents to be so proud of me and here I was going back empty-handed with nothing to show for the time I was in New York. As God would have it, the person sitting next to me on the flight back happened to be a pastor. We started talking, passing time on our four-hour flight and, eventually, we ended up on the conversation of time and restoration. He brought up the story of Rahab and gave me such an epiphany, and my life could never be the same."

Helen smiled, reminiscing.

"What is the first thing that comes to mind when you hear Rahab's name?" she asked Victoria, leaning back into the couch and making herself comfortable.

"Hmm," Victoria said, also getting comfortable on the couch. "I think of the savior of the Israelite spies."

"That is quite a rare answer. Usually the response is that she was a woman of the night, a harlot. The Bible called her a prostitute, which basically means she exchanged her body for money, food or whatever else she needed. With that scarlet letter on her chest, Rahab lived on the edge of society both physically as well as socially; she was on the lowest rung of the ladder, one step short of rejection. Her home was built right into the city wall. This was a strategic location for her in that the visitor could get easy access to her. But it was also strategic in the planning of the kingdom of Jericho – should there be an attack, the people that matter the least to the kingdom would be the first to die while the soldiers could care for the more important or wealthier folk in the inner city. Living on the wall, I assume that Rahab felt especially vulnerable. The talk of Israelites invading Jericho was no longer a rumor; she could feel the shift in the atmosphere that something life-changing was about to happen."

Helen looked at Victoria intently.

"How many times in your life have you felt the shift in the atmosphere because your faith went into overdrive when all your other faculties failed?" Helen asked, getting passionate about what she was trying to convey to Victoria.

"I am living by that, girl!" Victoria responded. "Hebrews 11:1 says, Now faith… not yesterday's faith or tomorrow's faith, but *now* faith – the faith I need to deal with what will move me into my prophetic destiny. It is the confidence in what we hope for and assurance about what we do not see. So as much as I struggle, that is what I live by."

"Exactly!" said Helen. "You have to pray with expectation and activate your faith and see God works. How many times have you had to walk by faith when the report you got was bad? Your faith stirred you up and you said I shall not die but live and declare the word of the Lord! How many times have you had to walk by faith when your employer said, 'Today is your last day of working here?' Your faith retorted, 'If God clothes the sparrows, aren't I more valuable than the sparrows?' He will take care of you because your employer is not your source! He is just a means to your blessing! How many times have you felt the shift in your spiritual atmosphere when the person you love with all your heart begins to act funny? Your faith stepped in and said God promised that He will never leave you nor forsake you! How many times have you felt the shift in the atmosphere when there was no food on the table and no money in your pocket, but then you knew there was the God who stated, 'I am your Jehovah Jireh – I can provide whatever you need.'

"You're preaching!" Victoria chimed in, getting as excited as Helen.

"You've got to be tested to be trusted. These are the tests that God uses to find out if you can be trusted with what he has in store for you."

Helen stood and started pacing.

"Do we have this confidence in God? That no matter what happens we are going to trust him? That though we are going against the rule of the majority we will remain in the will of God and do what He wants, come what may? Vicky, on that flight home and many times after I landed, I had to remind myself that I may not come out how I went in, but I will come out better than I was before. What happened to me here a year or so ago showed me that I am stronger, fitter and have gained strength where I didn't have strength before."

Tears started rolling down Helen's cheek as she testified. Victoria got up and went to stand next to her, offering her strength silently.

"Many times, people pass us over. We are deemed not intelligent, wealthy, worthy, beautiful or strong enough to be used. They would have done that to Rahab also but the omnipotent God was looking beyond her skin, beyond her situation and looking directly at her heart. He knew that she was someone that He could trust. She just had to be tested at the right time to prove her worth. Like Rahab, many of our lives are spinning out of control. The fact that we are still here isn't anything but a miracle."

As she listened, Victoria now knew why Helen showed up when she did.

"We often feel like we have lost or are losing our sanctification, our sanity and about to lose our lives. But God steps in and cuts that plan of the enemy to naught. You know God didn't allow me to die that day, that hour or even that minute when I lost all my hope. It was because He knew that I have greater work now and in the future to do. I remember the night you reminded me of this, when you spoke into my life."

Helen held Vicky's hand again and looked deeply into her eyes. The tears were falling, unencumbered now.

"He set you in my path that day, so I could get to this place of being totally surrendered to His will for my life, and I owe you so much, Vicky," said Helen.

"You don't owe me anything. That's what friends are for," Victoria said smiling.

Her eyes began to fill with tears again. Helen smiled at her friend and then did a dance to signify her joy while Victoria looked on, still smiling.

"What in Donald Trump's hairline is going on here?" Vicky's maid of honor, Sarai Parker, said as she entered the room.

"Just having church," Victoria said. "Something you will never understand."

"Excuse you?!" Sarai rejoined. "Let me inform you I go to church every Sunday and I can sha bab bab bad with the best of y'all."

"Since when do you go to church every Sunday?" Victoria interrogated. "The last time you went to church was at your christening service."

"See, that is how much you know, bestie," Sarai continued, coming over to where she and Helen stood laughing.

"Hi, Helen. Nice to see you. You look beautiful," Sarai rattled off, not stopping to take a breath in.

"Hi Sarai, nice to see you, too. Always the life of the party," she said, leaning into Sarai to kiss her cheek.

"You know how it is," replied Sarai, thrusting her right hand with her bouquet in the air, placing her left hand on her hip, then sticking her tongue out and gyrating.

Helen chortled loudly.

"No behavior, whatsoever," scolded Victoria. "And you go to church every Sunday? Where is this church?"

"Down the road from me," Sarai said. "It is one hour. I'm in, get my worship on and I am out. Not like when I come to your church. I have to carry my breakfast, lunch and dinner just to make it through that service."

Helen laughed even harder while Victoria huffed at Sarai with her arms crossed over her bosom.

"Anyway, I came to get the happy bride. They are ready for you," Sarai said, becoming serious.

"Victoria, you look beautiful, enjoy your day, hun. You deserved to be loved unselfishly and to be taken care of, finally! I will see you after the ceremony," Helen said, giving her friend a kiss and a tight squeeze before heading toward the door.

She exited and looked back, saying, "I will send the makeup artist in, to clean you up."

Victoria's mood returned to its somber disposition.

"You okay?" Sarai asked.

"Yes."

"You don't look like it."

"I am and I will be, hun,"

"Ok, I will let them know you need a few minutes," Sarai said, searching Vicky's face.

"Thank you, I appreciate you," Vicky said, turning away from Sarai to sit at the vanity table. She heard the door open and close as Sarai exited. She took one more look at her expression in the mirror, bowed her head and began to pray silently.

Father, I have mangled this situation very badly and I don't know how to fix it. Daddy, I apologize for not being brave and strong enough to live and speak my truth regardless of the feelings of others. I turn this situation and the remainder of this day over to you. If this is not your will for my life, please help me to get out of it. Whatever the reason you are allowing this, just like Rahab, I will follow wherever you lead. I know nothing happens to me without your consent; therefore, if you are allowing this, then it must be good for me. Thank you, Daddy, for loving me so much.

She was unaware when the makeup artist entered the room; however, she closed her prayer with a silent Amen and tilted her face toward the light when she heard her say, "Let's fix you."

"Let the day perish on which I was born, and the night that said, 'A man is conceived.' Why did I not die at birth, come out from the womb and expire?"

Job 3:3, 11

CHAPTER 20

Nick was so caught up in his reverie that he didn't see when the ring bearer walked past. He remembered when his fairytale came to an abrupt end over a year earlier. Victoria had gone out of town on business for her company. He knew she would not be back for at least a week. It was only day two and he was already missing her like crazy. During that time, Nick decided to break up with the other girl he was seeing. She was sweet, pretty, ebony-skinned and had a very nice smile. She also had a waiter's booty that kept men always looking her way. Even with all the attention that she garnered she was a nice person and didn't deserve to be treated so harshly. He didn't want to do it over the phone, so he decided to take her out for dinner at Red Lobster and break the news to her.

It would be three nights before Vicky came back into town. He could clear the air with the girl (for the life of him he couldn't remember her name offhand, all he knew was that it started with an N, he knew he would remember eventually) and then he would be able to concentrate on Vicky, plan a surprise welcome-back dinner for them and finally tell her how he felt. He was extremely excited to introduce Vicky to his "people," and see where things would go with them. The dinner was uneventful until the end. While leaving the restaurant, Nicole (yeah, that was her name) wanted a final goodbye kiss for old time's sake. Nick didn't really feel up to it, but she had been so understanding about the whole situation he felt the least he could do was give her that; it couldn't hurt.

Nicole clamped down on his mouth and kissed him like she was a woman who had been in the desert for days and he was her oasis. He put his hand on her hip to push her away, when he heard the gasp behind him. He felt it in his bones; he knew that kiss would cost him. He pulled away and turned around to meet the steely eyes of Victoria.

"Babe, it isn't what it seems," he began.

"Save it, Nick," Victoria stated, turning.

He lunged for her, grabbing her by the arm. Something in the depth of his soul said that if Victoria walked out of there he would need to move heaven and earth to have her walk back into his life.

"Please, baby, it is not what you think," Nick stated, his eyes pleading for her to understand.

"Not what I think?!" she said, her eyes cold. "Nicholas you are here sucking face with this person!" she pointed viciously in Nicole's direction. I have been gone for three days and this is what you do while I am away?"

She didn't wait for a response, snatching her arm away from him.

"I am done! I can't do this anymore. I don't deserve to be treated and disrespected like this. I have been nothing but loyal, faithful and true to you, but every time I turn around your actions and behavior have to be questioned. I can't live like this anymore."

Victoria finished softly.

"Obviously, I am not the woman you want, so I am going to leave you to the woman you do."

At that, the fight left Victoria's body and she turned back the way she had come.

Vicky was one for debating her point, but Nick saw the defeat in her eyes before she turned away. She was a proud woman; she would never fight over a man in public or even in private. She believed that each person was responsible for the choices they made and was accountable for the consequences. She walked away from him with her head held high even though he knew she must be hurting. It was only when she was out of sight did Nick realize that his sister Sarai was standing there.

"You idiot!" she declared, punching him on the arm.

Nicholas winced but not from the punch. Sarai hit like a girl, literally. The wince was not from the gut punch, but from the intensity of the accusation in her eyes.

"Sarai, I didn't do anything! I swear!" Nicholas countered. "Nicole kissed me, not the other way around."

"Really, Nicholas Parker?! You expect me to believe that? Even if that is true, you didn't stop her either, did you?" she asked.

Sarai only called him by his full name when she was really angry at him.

"Sarai, I swear on my life, I didn't do anything," Nicolas spat back.

People were beginning to look their way. Nicole was leaning against the wall, trying to conceal himself from Sarai, who kept hurtling daggers at her with her eyes.

"Nicholas, save it! Whether it is true or not, I am not the one that you need to convince," she said, turning and walking out the door.

Nick drew in a deep breath and turned to look at Nicole who had a look of sweet satisfaction on her face.

"Come on, Nicole I'll take you home," he said.

He would drop Nicole home and then swing by Vicky's apartment to talk to her. If she wasn't there he would give her a few days to cool down and then go find her. However, that would not be. Vicky didn't answer her phone or the doorbell when he rang that night. Several days later, her number was no longer in service. He tried to catch her before or after work but it seemed like she had disappeared into thin air. Sarai was just as cold to him. From the curses she flung at him sporadically, he learned from Sarai that Vicky had cut her trip short to be with him because she missed him so much. She knew how much he loved Red Lobster and had asked Sarai to drop her there so that she could get him some food before she went home. At least he knew now why she was there in the first place.

Finally, after about eight months, he heard Sarai and Vicky's other best friend, Brittany, talking about how Sarai had introduced Victoria to her boss and how they had hit it off. His own sister had betrayed him; she had introduced the love of his life to someone else. How could she? Didn't she know what this was doing to him? Nick felt like strangling his own sister but there were laws against things like that. It seemed like Vicky was moving on with her life. Nick decided to do likewise. He was a man — men didn't let women get the better of them. What would his boys say if they knew he was thinking of hunting her down and begging her to take him back? They would laugh at him. He couldn't have that. He was too proud for that. He picked up the phone and called Nicole. That was about 12 months ago.

After Victoria, Nick decided to keep everything above board where his relationships were concerned. Nicole turned out to be a sweet person, so sweet that it hurt his tooth a lot, but neither did he want to be alone right now. Nicole was becoming quite a permanent fixture to his life. All his exes knew about her. She had even met his mom. Everyone liked her with the exception of Sarai, who still believed that Victoria was the best thing that could have ever happened to him.

"What are you doing with this empty, bobble head doll, Nicky? You know you are not in love with this girl? Go to Victoria, apologize and tell her how you feel, Nicholas. Stop being so stubborn and proud. You are going to regret this," Sarai argued with him constantly.

Some days he was in agreement with Sarai but other days he was mad at Vicky; how could she walk away from what they had without a backward glance? Then he remembered the first time they had met - she had walked away from him without a backward glance that day, too.

I've learned; nothing is more expensive
than a missed opportunity

H. Jackson Brown Jr.

CHAPTER 21

Nick watched the events of the day through glazed eyes as he continued his reminiscing about life after Victoria. It was months before the void she left started slowly healing. He hadn't seen or heard from her in a while. Things between him and Nicole were going well. It was not as exciting as what he had with Victoria but it was comfortable. He wasn't going to be a fool like he was with Victoria and mess it up. It was a good relationship and he was going to maintain it the best way he knew how. He had learned to stop comparing the two after month eight. Nicole was her own person with her traits, likes and dislikes and he had to respect her for that. She did not challenge him too much and she was malleable. The sort of woman that did what you asked without too many questions. She wasn't exactly the ambitious type either, which was more of a con for him than it was a pro. She was no genius by any degree but she was competent in holding a conversation and could potentially become more, if she actually applied herself. However, her goal was to be the manager at the secretarial service where she worked. If she made it that high, there wasn't much farther for her to go. He couldn't understand that thinking, but he didn't belittle her dreams; they were hers, and she had all rights to do with them what she wanted. Her other goal seemed to be about pleasing him in every way and, so far, she was doing a great job, although sometimes it gnawed on his nerves. He now understood what Eddie Murphy as Prince Akeem in *Coming to America* felt like, when his father wanted him to marry the woman that he didn't love. It was just plain irritating.

He was managing his life a lot differently now and had started staying home on a Sunday instead of always working. One Sunday, his mom had dragged him out of the house with an invitation to attend church with her. He didn't have anything to do that day, *so why not?* he thought.

Inside the sanctuary, Nicholas sat there enthralled by the pastor who was talking about the wages of sin leading to death, and that there was a life after death.

"You would have to give an account for all that you have done with the life that you have been given. Right down to the very words that you use daily," the pastor exclaimed.

Nicholas was in shock; he had never heard this before. He listened some more as the pastor spoke about a God that loves us and didn't want for us to end up in a fiery hell, but gave his only son that we would have life everlasting. It was a God that unbeknownst to Nicholas had preserved him on his daily treks and covered him from seen dangers and those he was totally unaware of. We go about our day not even with a sense of gratitude. Nicholas had not accepted Him as his personal savior and had not committed his ways and life to him, yet He still kept him safe. Nicolas was pricked in his heart. He wanted what the pastor was offering. He wanted that everlasting life and relationship with God. When the altar call was made, he was the first one at the altar, surrendering his life to Christ. He was not one to cry publicly because he never knew black men to cry. Nonetheless, he stood in front of the altar unashamed, giving up every burden, disappointment and struggle he ever faced as a man and more so as a black man. His mom came and stood beside him, her tears rivaling him. He would later ask why she was crying so much and, she would say to him, it is because her prodigal son had finally come home.

He wasn't having sex with Nicole at the time but she was beginning to put pressure on him for them to sleep together. Her arguments for this would usually range from "Don't you find me sexy?" to "If you love me, you would show me you do." He was a changed man, those things didn't faze him anymore. He had nothing to prove to anyone. He tried explaining to her why he was not having sex with her and it had nothing to do with her. But, of course, that conversation went south and he realized, albeit too late, that he was defending himself about being with someone else. Her comment was "if you are not getting it here, you are getting it from somewhere else." He was not getting any from anywhere or anyone else. He was committed to keeping himself chaste until he got married. Most of his friends thought he had lost his mind – and maybe he had — a little but he was in so much of a better place mentally and emotionally. He didn't have to lie to cover another lie to cover another lie and so forth. And his days were not occupied with scheming how he was going to get in and out of some girl's underwear without too much drama from her or her family.

He still had desires but any time he felt desires coursing through his body, he handled it himself. When he started pleasuring himself, he had felt so guilty about it because all his life, he had been taught that masturbation was a sin. He decided to ask his Pastor Bob for insight into it.

"There is no direct answer from God about this," Pastor Bob said. "It is how you feel about what you're doing. If you feel like you're lusting, then that makes it a sin. If you are just getting some ease without projecting any real thought into it then I don't think that makes it a sin."

Nicholas was shocked.

"What about lust and Onanism?" Nicholas had queried.

He really didn't know what Onanism was but he had heard one of his friends, who was also saved, talking about it.

"Do you think about someone in particular when you masturbate?" Pastor Bob had asked?

"No, I just think about the release I need and it happens, I don't want to fornicate and it takes the edge off," said Nicholas with an honest shrug.

"Masturbation is a regular healthy part of human sexuality and you are not lusting as dictated in Matthew 5:27-28, which says *"You have heard that it was said, 'You shall not commit adultery.' But I say to you that everyone who looks at a woman with lustful intent has already committed adultery with her in his heart."*

Pastor Bob continued heartily, explaining that many people misconstrue what Onanism really is. While many have equated it to masturbation, Pastor Bob broke down the story of Onan, found in Genesis 38: 9 — *"But Onan knew that the child would not be his; so whenever he slept with his brother's wife, he spilled his semen on the ground to keep from providing offspring for his brother."*

"Onan was not masturbating. He was actually having sex with his late brother's wife and, in order to avoid raising children for his late brother, he did a corpus interruptus which is ejaculating outside of the vagina to avoid procreation of his brother's line. God was upset at the motives, not the act. Hence, God's punishment for it. There are a lot of so-called experts that hold a lot of rules and regulations against the people of God. However, where the Bible speaks, I speak, and where it is silent, I am silent. It is up to you. It is how you feel about what you are practicing. That is where the sin lies," Pastor Bob said.

Nicholas breathed an outward sigh of relief as Pastor Bob continued.

"What I am about to share is, not because I am perfect, guiltless, spotless or innocent, but I have made a commitment to God to obey Him regardless of the consequences that will come up on me. Christ declared '...he that loses his life for my sake shall surely find it, and thus as a willing vessel in the Potter's hand, so am I in the will of God.' Issues surrounding sex have plagued many a mighty men and nations of the world. Masturbation is the practice of sensual orgasm fashioned by self-stimulation for sexual awakening and pleasure. Every man does it at one point or the other. What I would tell you Nicolas is to do it in moderation. Don't let it consume you and you should be okay. God is not going to punish you for that," Pastor Bob said, leaning back into his chair and crossing his legs.

Nicholas had left that day feeling a little better about himself, because he wanted everything about his life to please God. But, he had nagging doubts about what he had heard. He confided in his friend Donald who was saved but went to a different church. When Donald heard what he was told, he sat with his mouth agape, and shook his head.

"Nick, I am not trying to dump on your pastor or what he told you, but I think that advice he gave was way off, bro," Donald said. "I used to have that problem too and I spoke with my youth pastor and he guided me through the Bible on this. I think you should speak with him."

"Oh, I would love to hear someone else's reasoning on this, from a scriptural context because I really want to do what is right," Nicolas said.

"Let me give Pastor James a call and see when he can meet with you," Donald said.

"Sure, that is cool," Nicholas responded.

Several hours later, Donald called Nicholas to tell him that Pastor James was available to meet that afternoon at his church. They had a youth event happening that evening but he had a couple of hours before that got underway, so he wanted to meet.

"Of course I can make it," Nicholas said.

He was stoked that a pastor who didn't know him had opened up his schedule to see him as urgently as he had. He asked his secretary to reschedule the remainder of his appointments for the afternoon and evening so he could address this situation.

Donald sent him the address and time and Nicholas showed up 30 minutes before the meeting so that he could get a lay of the land. From the outside, you could see that it was a beautiful edifice and that they took good care of the building. Nicholas was impressed. His mother always said cleanliness was next to godliness and, if this place was any indication, they were concerned about the things of God.

Nicholas buzzed the door to the church and a few minutes later it was opened by a man who could have been featured in an Armani catalog.

"Hi, I am Nicholas, I am looking for Pastor James," Nicholas said.

"Hey Nicholas, welcome. I am Pastor James," the man said, smiling and extending his hand.

"You're the pastor?" Nicholas said, baffled while shaking Pastor James' hand. Pastor James had a strong hand shake and Nicholas felt himself responding in kind.

Pastor James laughed loudly.

"Yes, Nicholas, I am one of the pastors here. Why does that surprise you?" he asked as he ushered Nicolas into the church.

"Well, you are so young. You're about my age," Nicholas responded.

Pastor James continued, laughing while they walked through what looked like a 300 plus auditorium on their way to his office.

"God calls us while we are young. Ecclesiastes 12: 3-7 from the Message Bible says *"In old age, your body no longer serves you so well. Muscles slacken, grip weakens, joints stiffen. The shades are pulled down on the world. You can't come and go at will. Things grind to a halt. The hum of the household fades away. You are wakened now by bird-song. Hikes to the mountains are a thing of the past. Even a stroll down the road has its terrors. Your hair turns apple-blossom white, adorning a fragile and impotent matchstick body. Yes, you're well on your way to eternal rest, while your friends make plans for your funeral. Life, lovely while it lasts, is soon over. Life as we know it, precious and beautiful, ends. The body is put back in the same ground it came from. The spirit returns to God, who first breathed it.*

"Wow..." Nicholas whispered. He was truly wowed that this man knew by heart such a long passage of poetically beautiful lines.

"1 Timothy 4:12," Pastor James continued. "*... Don't let anyone look down on you because you are young, but set an example for the believers in speech, in conduct, in love, in faith and in purity.*"

As they turned the bend, he said one last thing.

"So why not serve him while you can give him the best of you?" Pastor James asked.

Nicholas was stupefied and stopped in his tracks.

"Nicholas, are you okay?" Pastor James asked, facing him when he realized Nicholas was no longer in stride with him.

When Pastor James mentioned purity, Nick was shocked that the pastor was just spitting out his knowledge of the Bible like that. In that moment, he had also felt the conviction that his life was not pure and glorifying God. Purity, it seemed, was a big thing to God.

"Let's sit here and talk here. We should have the place to ourselves for another couple more hours," Pastor James said and signaled for Nick to sit in the first pew.

"Donald called and said that you were his friend and needed some spiritual guidance. He didn't go into details, but I felt the need to meet with you, so I made the time. How can I help you, Nicholas?" Pastor James asked.

"Recently I gave my life to God. It is one of the best decisions I have made and I am really enjoying the person that I am becoming. Prior to being saved, I was very sexually active. Now that I am saved I do not want to be a part of that lifestyle anymore so I have abstained from sex. However, I have found myself masturbating, and I want to know if this is okay. I spoke to the pastor at my church and he said there is nothing wrong with it if it is done in moderation. I've never been one to accept one person's word as law, Deuteronomy 19:15, the last clause says at *the mouth of two witnesses, or at the mouth of three witnesses, shall the matter be established*. So I want to hear what others have to say on this viewpoint because it has been bothering me immensely," Nicholas said without hesitation.

Pastor James looked at him, smiling.

"Using the scripture to back up what you are saying and in the right context. Brother, you are on your way," he stated with a grin.

Then, Pastor James took a serious tone.

"The issue that you are dealing with is one that has plagued humanity for a long time, especially godly men trying to do the right thing. In all honesty, Nicholas, there isn't anything in the scriptures that plainly addresses this issue of masturbation. There is not even a slight mention of it at all in the scripture. However, it speaks quite clearly on the issue of lust. Have you ever tried masturbation without lusting about something or someone?" Pastor James asked, making himself more comfortable on the pew.

"I don't think about anyone in particular, just how it makes me feel," Nicholas stated

"Really?!" Pastor James said, his left eyebrow cocked.

"Really." Nicholas replied.

"I find that quite hard to believe," Pastor James responded, looking intently at Nicholas.

"Really, that is it. Well, to begin, I thought about how my first girlfriend made me feel the first time I came," Nicholas stated.

"Aha!" Pastor James declared triumphantly. "People will give you any excuse for what they do with masturbation, but at the root of it is selfishness and lust. I have heard everything from, 'I do it to take the edge off,' I do it so that I would not fornicate or commit adultery.' For those that are married, they don't consider it a sin at all. Why? Because Pastor James I am thinking about my wife/husband," Pastor James stated passionately, counting them off on his fingers.

"Russell Willingham's book "*Breaking Free*" states that masturbation disturbs, intrudes, and upsets the Bible's concept of sexuality. You may ask why this is so. It is due to the fact that when the Bible speaks of sex, it communicates an amalgamation between a man and woman. It's an experience that should be shared and that idyllically breaks down our selfishness, transports us out of ourselves and presents the real person to the mind/soul of another. Masturbation is extremely self-absorbed. The central focus on masturbation is self. It is all about how it makes *you* feel, *your* wants, *your* needs, *your* desires instead of thinking about someone else's needs and desires. Thus, when you do get married and in a relationship with someone who is depending on you to care about their needs, wants and desires, you are unable to come (no pun intended) up to the mark, since you are still trying to get your own first and you leave the other person unfilled."

Nicholas found himself nodding in agreement to what Pastor James was saying. There was something about what the man of God was saying that reverberated within him. He felt like he was getting the truth as God intended.

"Masturbation skews one's assessment, interpretation and understanding of sex, into being about our pleasure and a quick fix rather than the focus being on giving and intimacy in a committed marriage connection. Eduardo J. Echeverria, a philosophy professor at Sacred Heart seminary who writes about sexual ethics, wrote that the good of sexuality comes from the fact that it bonds two people and is tied to baby-making. Masturbation violates both of those things. Echeverria went further and said that masturbation can lead to using pornography or helping someone avoid fixing any sexual problems in their marriage. Regardless of the fact that it feels good, it is meaningless. Echeverria also said that adultery can produce pleasure and so can pedophilia. But are they right? Human sexuality has a nature, and it's toward union and the good of the other."

Pastor James took a breath, praying that he wasn't going too fast for Nicholas.

"Masturbation also acts as a conduit for the pursuit of other sexual immorality and demonic possession. When we open our lives to certain things that are not godly, it allows other things to manifest in our lives. Matthew 12: 43-45 says *when an impure spirit comes out of a person, it goes through arid places seeking rest and does not find it. Then it says, 'I will return to the house I left.' When it arrives, it finds the house unoccupied, swept clean and put in order. Then it goes and takes with it seven other spirits more wicked than itself, and they go in and live there.*

And the final condition of that person is worse than the first. That is how it will be with this wicked generation. Don't get it twisted, Nicholas. The world is telling us that these things are okay because it is part of our sexual make up and that the white man's God made these rules to keep us in bondage. The Bible says that Jesus walked amongst us and that he became flesh. Ask yourself this question. Do you think that Jesus masturbated to take the edge off? When we are in positions that require us to act as Christians and we refer to WWJD, we have to think of that also in the case of masturbation. Can you see Jesus doing this? Christianity is defined as disciples of Christ, which means we do what he does. If you can't imagine him going down this route, then why would you?"

Pastor James went on.

"Sex is a beautiful thing that God created. But, as with anything, when taken out of its true context and overused, it becomes an issue. There is a song "Kill my flesh" by Chevelle Franklin that brings back to memory my scripture devotion for today. And knowing that there are no coincidences with God, I am going to share it with you."

Pastor James told Nicholas about a passage from Jeremiah 7. *Will you steal and murder, commit adultery and perjury, burn incense to Baal and follow other gods you have not known, and then come and stand before me in this house, which bears my Name, and say, "We are safe"—safe to do all these detestable things?*

"How often are we as Christians guilty of this? Doing whatever we feel to do because of the option of grace? How often do these things become a part of our lives because of the need to impress someone or compromise for someone? How often are we going to cheat on that one person that has never cheated on us yet remains ever vigilant and waiting for us to come back? I was pricked to my core at the conclusion of the scripture."

Pastor James encouraged Nicholas to read the scripture passage himself to see what we could learn on his own.

"You have the spirit of God and it will direct you the right way. Your heart will be pricked when you are erring. I do not condemn you. But if your heart condemns you, your God is still bigger than your heart, "Pastor James concluded.

Nicholas sat there in awed silence, experiencing the reassurance of the Holy Spirit. He knew what Pastor James was saying was true. His last words were, to him, more like 'a-word-to-the-wise...' He was hearing what God wanted him to hear in the fullness of the truth. Psalms 119:6 says *Wherewithal shall a young man cleanse his way? by taking heed thereto according to thy word.* He realized that it was the Holy Spirit that had made him push to find out more about this because what he was initially being told did not line up with the true word of God. An intense love for God filled Nicholas as he sat there. Pastor James prayed with him and ended the conversation, stating that he had to get ready for the youth program in a few minutes. He invited Nicholas to stick around, but Nicholas said he couldn't stay. So, they exchanged numbers and Nicholas promised to call if he had any more questions.

Nicholas left that evening more determined in his heart that nothing and no one would change his mind and alter his love for God. If he knew this was how his life was going to be, he would have gotten saved much earlier. He had a hunger for the understanding of God. He was ardent about his relationship and he wanted nothing to stand in the way of that. It didn't mean that he was perfect. In fact, most days he struggled to do the right thing and maintain his faith. But he was getting his life right.

He promised himself that soon he was going to make a woman very happy that she had chosen him as her mate.

"Women have so much power that they are unaware of. They don't know that in the dating process they are the one that calls the shots of what they will allow or not. They settle for any old joker because they don't want to be alone," he had told Sarai when they were younger.

But Sarai had taken that bull by the horn and ran with it. She would hardly submit to any man in her life, although that was an extreme worldview. Love was a shared road that a man and woman walked together. If Sarai didn't rethink that route she was on, she was going to end up all alone because, at the end of the day, no man wants a woman to bully or boss him around. Yes, for independence. Yes, for feminism. But those have their place and time. He prayed that God would send Sarai a man that would be able to handle her and show her that love, monogamous love is a beautiful thing worth having. He knew that now. He just wished he had admitted to himself when he had Victoria in his life because, even though he was with Nicole, his mind always drifted to Victoria and played the game of what if.

For everything there is a season, and a time for every matter under the heaven.

Ecclesiastes 3:1

CHAPTER 22

Nicholas was totally caught up in his musing by this point. He started remembering Nicole's birthday and how he had decided to take her out to his favorite restaurant in The City. He knew she would like it; she liked whatever he liked, it seemed. He wanted it to be special so he had made the reservation two weeks in advance. He had told Nicole that it was a dress-up affair. But when he picked her up, he couldn't help but think, what the hell?! Nicole was wearing a tight black top that exposed her protruding boobs along with tight spandex pants and some strappy sandals. She looked good but he didn't think the outfit was appropriate for the restaurant. It also made him feel overdressed, but Nick kept his opinion to himself.

They arrived at the restaurant with plenty of time to spare before they would have to be seated at their table. Upon entering the restaurant, Nick heard his name and recognized Richard as the caller.

After his break from Vicky, Nick had spent a lot of time playing ball at the gym. It was there he had met Richard. They had become fast friends, often chilling out, playing basketball, football, and billiards while swapping college stories. Nick liked Richard; he was a cool guy for the most part.

Nick grabbed Nicole's hand and made his way toward the table where Richard sat with a lady. At the gym, the men always teased Richard about the foxy lady he had. But for some reason her name never came up and he had never met her. *Maybe tonight I'll finally get to meet the mysterious woman,* he thought. But knowing Richard, he knew she could be one of his many mistresses that he kept hidden. Nick had played those games. He saw the signs in Richard and knew the kind of dirt he was doing. But it wasn't any of his business, so he let him be; Richard would learn his lesson eventually. Nick hoped he learnt it sooner rather than later. Those games usually came back to bite you when you least expected it.

Richard got up to give him a hug and thump on his back then said, "this is my fiancée." Nick had started to question *fiancée*? He never thought that Richard would be with one woman, much less introduce a fiancée. When he glanced at the woman sitting at the table, his world came to a startling halt.

No, it couldn't be! Impossible! His brain screamed at him. Sitting there was Victoria, his Victoria. She had lost weight but she was still as beautiful as ever.

"Nice to meet you," Nick croaked.

"Likewise," she said as she shook his hand slightly and then started to pull away.

Nick couldn't let her hand go, not just yet. There was a bolt of electricity running through him again. He couldn't help himself from tightening his clasp when Richard said that the wedding would be in the next two months. He saw her visible wince as the promise ring he had given her two years ago bit into her flesh. If she was going to marry Richard, why was she still wearing it? He let go of her hand and remembered to introduce Nicole, after all she was the reason that they were there. He saw Victoria give her the once-over. The telltale arch of an eyebrow told him she wasn't too pleased nor impressed by what she saw. However, she was too much of a lady to say anything at all.

Richard wanted them to sit with them at the table. Nick wasn't exactly thrilled at the idea but the fact that Victoria spoke out against it raised his ire and he decided to sit with them. He wanted to know what had made her accept Richard's proposal. Every thought about making this night memorable for Nicole had flown out the window as soon as he had seen Victoria. He had to admit to himself that he was wrong; she still held the ability to mesmerize him. That night the food tasted like chalk to him. All he could see was the ring sparkling, mocking him from her finger as she kept a cool composure. Never once did she look at him throughout the night. She ate with poise and answered all questions short and concisely.

Richard scooted closer and kissed her on her neck. Nick clenched the glass he was holding. It broke apart in his hand spilling the red wine on the virgin white tablecloth. "Are you okay?" Victoria asked with concern.

The fact that she was worried about him tugged at his heartstrings and their eyes locked. Time stood still for him and he remembered all the reasons why she was the only one that had stolen his heart. It was moments like this when she was concerned for his well-being even though he was a grown man.

"Let me see," Nicole said, breaking the spell.

"Nick, you are bleeding," she said as he looked down to see the deep gash in his palm.

"We better take care of that," said Nicole, escorting him to the bathroom. When they came back, Richard was still there but Victoria had left, complaining of a headache. He hadn't seen her again since then.

Nick came back to reality as the tune "Here comes the bride" resounded throughout the church. There she stood, leaning on her brother's arm. Her face was covered by a translucent veil, but he could see her perfectly. She stole his breath away. Tears dampened her lashes and ran down her cheek. She was crying because she was happy she was getting married.

"Damn it!" Nick cursed under his breath.

She held his gaze for a moment as she passed and Nick knew he could not watch her marry another man. She was the missing piece in his life. He knew it was crazy but he couldn't live without her in his life. He just couldn't. He'd be damned if he let another man have her.

If he couldn't have her, then no one else would. He vowed silently and turned to see her brother handing her over to Richard. Nick's jaw ticked and he clenched and unclenched his fist.

"This new subterfuge is, of course, calculated to deceive the simple and innocent into thinking that the matter is settled."

Martin Luther

CHAPTER 23

Richard glanced at the gold Rolex resting comfortably on his left wrist and sighed. It was only 2 p.m. The wedding was scheduled to start at 2:30 pm and he was getting antsy for it to start and end. He waited quite a while for this and he didn't think he could wait any long to get to the celebratory session of this event. However, time was surely dragging her scrawny legs today.

He stood at the front of the church, his hands in the pocket of his white Armani pants. The tux that he had brought for the occasion fit him as though it was made for him — and it was. As the center of attention today, he had to look his best – you never knew who would be looking at you. First impressions were lasting and he wanted to be remembered as being the dashing groom. He smiled. He knew he looked good -- well, better than good. He was the epitome of sharp.

He brought his attention back to the audience. The church was filling up quickly. At one point, he thought it couldn't hold any more people but they kept on coming, and the ushers seemed to find space to fit everyone comfortably. A few people stood over at the side table signing the guest registry book. The ushers were passing out fans and nick knacks for the wedding. The door opened and more people poured in. He shook his head. Who were all these people by the way? He didn't recall approving a full church. He thought he told Victoria only 100 people could come? This looked closer to 350 people. He tried to find a face in the crowd that he knew but he didn't recognize anyone.

He looked out over the packed room and did a quick calculation of what this wedding was going to cost him and he sighed. Some things were just unavoidable when you wanted something badly enough. Spending money was one of those things. Good thing he had plenty of it. He wanted Victoria Marshall, and he was going to have her by any means necessary. Sacrificing a couple thousand dollars was not going to hurt him at all. And, at the end of it, Victoria Malcolm would be his. He smiled to himself.

He knew Victoria didn't want to marry him. He knew that from the get go. You didn't get to be where and who he was by sheer luck. You learn to read people, scheme and manipulate them to ensure that what you want, you get; and that is exactly what he had done. He knew if he had asked her to marry him in private, she would have turned him down flatly. But she would not risk embarrassing him in public, so he made his play in a crowded restaurant to ensure her answer. And just as planned, she had said yes.

He gave himself an imaginary pat on the back for his acting role. Playing the role of the besotted, adoring fiancé was quite thrilling. He deserved an Oscar for his performance. Well, all of it was not a lie - he had to admit. Victoria was definitely getting under his skin. If he was honest with himself, he really liked her a lot. He could probably even be in love with her, too, but he didn't know what that was like so he couldn't call it that. He knew she was a constant staple in his mind and he was very happy to hear from her and see her. He even found himself looking forward to going to her boring church and having her introduce him as her fiancé. The last time he had gone with her, her pastor made them stand up together to announce their upcoming nuptials, then invited them to come to the altar so that prayers could be offered for them.

Victoria had turned beet red by the attention but Richard loved it. He even bowed toward Victoria a couple of times for good measure, as the people cheered. Church people were so gullible, they ate up that sort of husband-loving their wife/fiancée gesture. As they walked back to their seats, Richard overheard one of the single women telling her friend, "Victoria is so lucky. I pray God blesses me with a man like him. My own personal Boaz." Richard smiled at the compliment. After the service, as they were making their way to the parking lot, people kept coming up to them to offer congratulatory remarks. Man, did he love being the center of attention.

As they drove home that day, Victoria tried to talk to him about the wedding but he knew she was trying to get out of it. He created another emergency at the office and left. There was no way that he was going to let her out of this deal – well, not until he had his way with her. He would make sure he had a good time with her and then divorce her. With his wealth and network, he was sure that he could get that done in a month. However, if marrying her was what it took to get what he wanted, he was willing to make the sacrifice. Plus, one or more of his lovers was waiting in the wings for him, even with Victoria as his wife.

His modus operandi was to start a relationship before the other one he was in had matured – which oftentimes meant, you introduce your main squeeze to your side chicks. He already introduced several of them to Victoria as friends of his. She would not suspect a thing when he decided to hang with them, or give her the excuse that they needed help with something late at night or for a lengthy period of time during the day.

These women were fine with her being his wife. Some of them were also married and had no plans to leave the security of their own marriages. They just wanted a little fun on the side to distract from the monotony of their humdrum lifestyle. They were not willing to rock the boat; they just wanted whatever he could offer them. Therefore, it worked out for all parties involved.

He looked over the crowd again and saw Nicholas Parker enter the church with the big booty girl from the restaurant, and he smiled sarcastically. He had invited Nicholas to the wedding because he knew Nicholas had feelings for Victoria. It was sort of an *'I have what you want, sir, and there is nothing you can do about it'* jab at Nick.

Oh yeah, he knew about Nicholas and Victoria! He had a private investigator dig into Victoria's past after Nicholas' reaction to him kissing her on the neck and her abrupt departure from the restaurant when he got hurt. He suspected they knew each other. Thus when the PI came back with the information, he had a golden ticket to rub salt in open wounds and he definitely was not going to pass on that opportunity.

This should be fun, he thought. He never really cared for Nicholas. There was just something about him that set his teeth on edge. But most of the other guys liked Nicholas a lot, always talking about how cool, smart and kind he was. So, he stayed in the loop. You never knew when you would need a good lawyer. Apparently, Nicholas was one of the top lawyers at his firm, so Richard was keeping him close just in case.

Richard was so deep in thought that he did not hear Sean come up from behind. He jumped when he felt a hand on his shoulder. He turned swiftly toward the person.

"Wow!" laughed Sean, jumping back.

"It is only me, your awesome best man," he said, smiling and adjusting his black tie playfully. His white teeth flashed brightly against his dark skin as he smiled broadly. He stood next to Richard and they both were the same height. Whereas Richard wore a White Armani suit with black trimmings and vest, Sean's grey Armani suit was trimmed with white. For those who didn't know who the groom was, they tried to figure out which one of them was the lucky person.

"A bit jumpy there, my brother. Are you okay?" Sean queried, still smiling.

"I am okay."

"Don't worry, Richard. Everyone gets nervous," Sean said, pounding him on the shoulder.

"I'll take your word for it, seeing as I have never done this before," Richard said.

"Trust me. You will be all right. You are nervous now, but as soon as you see Victoria, nothing else will matter other than making her your wife and getting to spend the rest of your life with her. I know this because that was how I felt on the day of my wedding," Sean stated, getting serious.

Richard breathed in deeply and shook out his hands as he released the air from his lung. Sean laughed heartily.

"All right, Mayweather! It is not a boxing match. You are going to be okay."

"I know. I am just a little nervous here. I want this to be over."

"It will be. Five more minutes before we start and then everything will be a blur and you will come back to earth. You will be a married man with a wife," Sean stated, with his hand resting on Richard's shoulder.

"I want to let you know that I am proud of you, Richard," Sean said, getting serious and staring Richard squarely in the eyes.

"You are?"

"Yes I am. Victoria is a beautiful person, both in and out. You are quite the lucky man. You did good Richard, really well. I was beginning to worry about you, bro, thinking that you would forever be a dog and never settle down. When you said you met someone and you asked her to marry you, I thought you would just sleep with her and let her go. I am so glad you're proving me wrong."

Richard swallowed the lump that formed in his throat and said, "Thank you, Sean. That means a lot to me."

"You are welcome. Victoria is good for you and you will not find another like her. Cherish what you have because women like her don't come our way very often."

"I hear you, bro, and I will."

"I am here if you need anything, Richard. All you need to do is ask. I'm only a phone call away. "

"I know." Richard said.

"Alright fellas, please take your places." said the minister. "We are about to start."

*Karma (car-ma) **is** a word **meaning** the result of a person's actions as well as the actions themselves. It **is** a term about the cycle of cause and effect. According to the theory of **Karma**, what happens to a person, happens because they caused it with their actions.*

CHAPTER 24

On shaky legs and with guttural sobs, Victoria arrived at the front of the church. She was a total wreck.

Pull yourself together girl, she admonished herself.

Who told you to say yes in the first place, eh? You had ample opportunity to call it off, but you are too much of a punk to do so, always caring about others' feelings rather than your own. See where it has gotten you? People will always have something to say, but you spent so much of your time skipping on their opinions that you are stuck here. Now you are going to pay for it for the rest of your life. Foolish girl! Now, suck it up and man up. Nicholas is here; you don't want to embarrass yourself any further than you already have, she argued with herself.

As she looked at the minister, she uttered one final desperate prayer.

"Father, please help me."

"Who gives this woman to be married to this man?" asked the officiating minister.

"I do," her brother John said.

Victoria's hand was passed over to Richard and John walked away.

"Ecclesiastes 4:12-14 says, *'and if one prevails against him, two shall withstand him; and a threefold cord is not quickly broken.'* This simply means that a person standing alone can be attacked and defeated, but two can stand back-to-back and conquer," said the minister. "Three is even better, for a triple-braided cord is not easily broken. That is what is happening here today. These two separate lives have decided along with the Holy Spirit to join forces and support each other, through the good and the bad...."

"Are you okay, Nick?" Nicole asked.

Nick did not hear a word that she said. Although his eyes were glued to the front of the church where Victoria and Richard stood, his mind was far away. Memories of Victoria and him flooded his mind: Vicky and him in cooking class - they were asked to bake a cake. Nick, not knowing anything about baking, ended up with most of the flour on his person. He looked like Casper with only his eyes being seen. Victoria could not contain her laughter and laughed till her side hurt. She had ended up making the cake by herself as he cleaned flour out of his hair, ears, nose and beard (the first and last beard he had ever grown). That memory was soon replaced by their first kiss. It was under a full moon and they had had a picnic in the park that night; they were sitting across from each other and having a ball in each other's company. She would catch him staring every now and again and would ask him what he was staring at. And, he was honest when he responded with, "The most beautiful woman I have ever seen."

She had chuckled and dubbed him a Casanova because of all the compliments. She had leaned forward at the same time he had to retrieve a strawberry and their hands touched. Nick had felt that jolt of electricity again and looked at Vicky. It seemed that she had felt it this time too and was gazing into his eyes.

It seemed that the world stood still for a while and Nick knew he wanted to taste those luscious lips to see if they were as soft and succulent as they looked. He had leaned into her and she did not move. She closed her eyes and Nick tasted her. He knew he would never get tired of drinking from her lips. They were just as he thought they would be with the added bonus of the tangy taste of strawberry. The next memory was of them splashing each other at the beach. Nick was an excellent swimmer but Victoria was partly a fish, it seemed. She loved the water and any opportunity she had, she could be found at the beach. That day she had scared the crap out of him. They were swimming when she started struggling; apparently, she had a cramp in her legs. She was too far away from him when she went under. He had dived where she had gone under, but he could not see her. He came up gasping for air and looked around to see if she had come up but she was not there. He was too far from shore to get any help right now. He started calling her name but there was no response. He was frantic with worry and he felt a hollow pit beginning to form in his stomach; he could not lose her like this. He went down again but he had to come up for air. He went down several times but no Vicky. His lungs began to burn and he came back up with his heart in his throat. He began to swim for shore to get help when he felt something grab his leg and pulled him under. He began to fight and kick. He came up sputtering and there was Victoria laughing at him. He dunked her and held her there for a minute - relief, anger, laughter and tears battling inside him. He let her go and she came up sputtering and laughing.

"Don't ever do that to me again," he chided her that day. "You scared me half to death." All laughter completely disappeared from her face when she saw that he was serious. She promised not to do that again, wrapped her legs around him and kissed him like there was no tomorrow.

The last memory broke him and caused him tear up. It was five months before they broke up. It was three in the morning and his phone rang. Half asleep, he answered. It was Victoria. Instantly, he knew something was wrong. Her voice was hollow and low, it sounded like she was crying. Sleep immediately left him when she said, "I need you."

He knew her enough to know that she did not ask for anything so if she was calling him at that time it must be for something very important. Nick made record time getting to her apartment. When he walked into the apartment, Vicky was curled up in a ball on the couch crying. He went over to her and picked her up as if she weighed no more than a child. He sat on the couch with her in his lap and waited for the torrent of tears to pass so he could find out what was wrong.

Her arms around his neck were like a vice but he knew he would survive until she was ready to talk. Through her tears, he learnt a drunk driver had run a red light and killed her father. Her dad had died instantly. He knew how close they were and it tore at his heart to see her like this. It seemed like hours they sat like that before her tears subsided. Her quiet breathing signaled to Nick that she was asleep. He picked her up, took her to the bedroom and placed her in bed. His shirt was soaked from her tears, so he took a quick shower and got into bed. She instinctively curled into him. It was that night that Nick knew beyond any doubt that she was for him; she had gotten under his skin and made him fall in love with her. She was like the air he breathed.

Nicholas got up and walked out of the church. He couldn't stay there and watch Victoria marry another man, but he didn't have the right to interrupt her life. He had taken advantage of her when she was his and now he was dealing with the consequences of his actions. He stood on the sidewalk taking deep breaths and trying to calm himself. The sound of the church's door opened, causing him to turn around. Nicole was standing there looking at him with tears in her eyes.

"You still love her, don't you?" she asked softly.

"Yes, I do Nicole." he said. "I am sorry that I can't tell you differently. It would be unfair for me to continue this relationship with you, knowing how I feel. I have to sort myself out, if I am to move on from her."

He walked toward her and took her hands in his.

"You are a beautiful and kind person. You deserve someone who will love you totally and right now I am not that person because my heart belongs to someone else. It took this occasion for me to see that. I was not trying to lead you on. I did not know the full extent of what she meant to me until this moment. I am sorry, Nicole, I really am. I never meant to hurt you."

He finished, using his thumb to wipe away her tears.

"I know," she said, holding his hand to her face. "You are a good man, Nicholas. I am just sorry you couldn't be my man."

She kissed his palm as she said it.

He passed her the handkerchief he had in the breast pocket of his shirt, and watched her clean herself up. She was a beautiful woman, but not the woman for him.

"Take my car, I'll send someone to get it later," he said and escorted her to his car.

He opened the driver's door and helped her in. He passed her the keys.

"Be careful. Drive safely…and I will talk to you soon," Nicholas finished.

He stood on the sidewalk, his hand in the pocket of his Armani suit, watching Nicole drive away. He felt at peace even though he was alone. This was the first time in a long time that he didn't have a woman in his life that was hoping and expecting much more from him than he could give. He was truly all alone but he wasn't lonely. He stood there in the stillness, talking to God and expressing his gratitude.

He began to walk to the street to hail a cab when he heard shots ring out from within the church.

"Vicky!" he shouted then sped toward the entrance of the church.

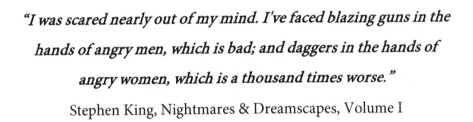

"I was scared nearly out of my mind. I've faced blazing guns in the hands of angry men, which is bad; and daggers in the hands of angry women, which is a thousand times worse."

Stephen King, Nightmares & Dreamscapes, Volume I

CHAPTER 25

"Dearly beloved, we are gathered here today, in the sight of God to join this woman, Victoria Angel Malcolm, and this man, Richard Lorenzo Washington, in the bonds of holy matrimony."

These were the words that brought Victoria back to reality.

"The bond of marriage is sacred and God in His infinite wisdom knew that man should not be alone, hence he made woman from the very rib of man. So it is the duty of man to love, honor, cherish, protect and, leaving all else, cling to the woman he has chosen to marry," said the minister.

The church was silent as he continued to pronounce the blessing of God upon the couple. Victoria was not sure but it seemed to her that the minister was rambling. Well, as far as she was concerned, he could ramble on for the entire day. As long as it warded off the "I now pronounce you husband and wife" bit, she did not mind at all.

This was supposed to be her wedding, a day when she should be her happiest, yet there she was dreading those words. Everything except her was perfect. She did not have to do anything for this wedding; Richard had made sure that she had gotten the best of everything. She had been brought to the church in a white horse-drawn carriage, and at the entrance of the door had been trumpeters to signal her arrival. Each guest had been given instructions written on glass to say where the reception would be held after the ceremony. Richard did not want any party crashers, so no one knew where the reception would be held until they arrived at the church. Unless you had an invitation, you couldn't get into the ceremony. Security was tight. Victoria didn't think that so much security was necessary. Richard was innately paranoid but this was taking it to a whole other level, but she couldn't be bothered with that right now. She had to make it through this day and she was still praying for a miracle.

The church itself was breathtaking; each column had been expertly wrapped in gold and white silk sheets with crimson red roses down the middle. Each pew was joined by the same gold and while silk draping; crimson red, pink and white roses embraced each other at the center of the pew. Smartly dressed livery attendants seated each guest. Each guest, upon their arrival, was presented with a gold-encrusted handcrafted oriental fan that bore a distinguished picture of her and Richard. The programs were written on parchment in the form of scrolls, the letters in gold ink with their faces serving as the watermark.

The arch, under which she stood, had been specifically built to accommodate Richard's height and had been flown in from Italy along with the miniature wooden bongs that were filled with bejeweled confetti. The ivory long-stemmed roses that were interwoven in the arch were flown in from Paris and had only arrived this morning. His and her families were given pink, red and white diamond lapel pins to wear to the wedding. At the reception hall, awaiting them would be sushi, caviar, shrimp, lobster, and all manner of seafood. Food and drinks galore! At the end of the night, each guest would go home with a bottle of champagne and a gift bag worth $1,000 each. The entertainment for the night would be international soul singer Sade. During her break, the sounds of a live soca band would fill the air. No expense had been spared for this day.

"If anyone knows a just cause why these two should not be married please speak now or forever hold your peace," Victoria heard.

The place was as silent as a tomb. Vicky looked around to see if anyone would say anything. She saw Nick rising and her breath caught, but he only turned and walked out the door. Nicole followed after him. Victoria's heart sank and she turned to face Richard with tears streaming down her face.

The remainder of the ceremony passed in a blur. She did not remember when they exchanged the rings or when Richard lifted the veil to kiss her or even when she signed the marriage certificate. She just wanted everything to be over. She was beginning to have a huge headache and she felt like she was going to throw up.

Richard grabbed her and twirled her around. She could not help laughing. He was such a big kid when he wanted to be.

"How do you feel, Mrs. Washington?" he asked.

"I feel okay," Vicky responded, in all honesty, placing her arms through his.

She was beginning to feel better after that shared laughter. He really was not a bad man. He had treated her very well ever since they had been together, and she hadn't had a cause to worry about him.

"Let's do this, Mrs. Washington," Richard said as they started walking down the aisle toward the exit.

Numerous people were stopping them on their way out. Their congratulations were interspersed with warm, tight hugs and big kisses. People were crying and laughing simultaneously. Victoria felt the love that was being poured out to them. She could not help but smile. The joy from the attendees was contagious. They were almost at the exit when this elegantly dressed lady stepped toward them. She was dressed in a white, strapless gown that hugged her like a second skin.

White at someone else's wedding? That is so uncouth, thought Victoria.

But she wore it well, Victoria had to admit. The woman was her height with an oval face, and she was beautiful. She actually reminded Victoria of the singer, songwriter and actress LeToya Luckett. Her makeup was flawless, blended perfectly into dewy almond skin. Her honey blond hair was pulled back in a ponytail at the nape of her neck, emphasizing and elongating its slender form. Victoria didn't know her but obviously Richard did because he froze in his tracks.

"Nisha, what are you doing here?" Richard asked, looking around.

"Surprised to see me, Richard?" she asked coldly. "I am sure you are, but I came to pay tribute to you and the beautiful bride."

The woman spoke with condescension in her tone.

"How did you know I was getting married today?" Richard asked, trying to put himself between Victoria and Nisha.

"That is for me to know and for you to find out Richard, darling," she said with saccharine sweetness, moving closer to Victoria.

Victoria looked around. Everyone was watching the scene unfold. Victoria noticed Sarai, Helen and Brittany inching their way toward her. She shook her head at them in the negative, hoping that they would stay where they were, but they kept making their way in her direction.

"So, you are Victoria, the woman that Richard decided to marry," Nisha sneered, looking Victoria up and down with disdain. "You're pretty, but then again we are all pretty."

She looked Richard up and down and casually walked around the couple.

"Richard, Richard, Richard. You certainly do have a type."

Richard's eyes followed her warily. Victoria could sense his apprehension and she began to feel uneasy, herself. Most of the guests had stepped back to give them room, but no one had left the church. All eyes and phones were riveted toward them. Victoria didn't like being the center of attention in this context and decided to try and diffuse the situation.

Victoria spoke up.

"You have the privilege of knowing who I am, but I have not had the honor of meeting you."

"Oh, she speaks!" Nisha said, acting shocked.

"I do it every now and again," Victoria said, smiling sincerely.

Nisha stared at Victoria with a steely gaze for a few minutes.

"I am Nisha Freeman, I was Richard's fiancée for two years up until today. We both have the same ring," she spat with venom, presenting her left hand.

Her manicured French tip nails were immaculate, and she stuck out her ring finger so that the platinum ring with the black diamond winked laughingly in the sunlight.

There was an audible gasp throughout the church.

"Is that true, Richard?" Victoria asked.

"It is not what she is saying," Richard began.

"Stop the lies! For once in your wretched life, stop lying. You don't get to weasel your way out of this one," Nisha screamed.

She continued in a blind rage.

"I am tired of your deception, manipulation and your lack of accountability. Today, that all stops. You wasted three years of my life and then you tossed me aside like I was yesterday's news?! Like I didn't matter. Like I was not someone's daughter or that I didn't have feelings? All I ever did was love you. Undeserving of it as you were, I loved you. I loved you more than I loved myself and this is how you embarrass me, by not being man enough to tell me that you no longer want me?"

She yelled with tears streaming down her face.

As Victoria watched Nisha's public breakdown, her own eyes filling and overflowing. She felt the hurt emanating from her, and her heart ached for the woman.

"Do you know where he told me he was going today?" she asked, looking at Victoria. "He said he was going away for a business trip. He had a huge deal for his company that he couldn't get out of. But I knew he was lying. This dirty piece of nobody who thinks only of himself was lying again. But it's all good."

She wiped the snot and tears from her face with the back of her left hand.

"You don't deserve me, I am better than this."

Her shoulders slumped as she spoke.

"You will get what is coming to you, Richard. You will suffer for all the people that you hurt," she said and turned to walk away.

"I will never suffer!" Richard shouted at her back, releasing Victoria's hand and taking a step forward.

Nisha stopped walking and Victoria saw her body visibly stiffen as her head came up. She turned to face them. Her eyes fixated on Richard.

As if a lion who was just baited by a hyena, Richard started in on her.

"You barge in here behaving like you're some big deal, and I owe you something? I don't owe you anything. In fact, if I start collecting from you, you would owe me for the rest of your life to pay off the debt... after everything I've ever given to you or that you begged or borrowed from me. You should have stayed your uppity behind at home," Richard spat venomously.

The vein in the front of his forehead amplified itself, signaling his anger.

"When I met you, you were a mere paralegal, nothing worth bragging about, with your discount clothing and drugstore makeup. I made you who you are. I introduced you to the high life. I gave you a wardrobe without holes and rips. I drenched you in expensive perfumes and threw out your cloying, outdated White Diamonds set. I know your gold digging type. You're nothing to brag about. Anyone can have you, once they have some money," he continued, spewing viciously.

Victoria stood mummified, looking at Richard and the immaculate mask he wore coming undone in the presence of everyone. All eyes and ears were glued to him. Victoria could see a few people recording the scene while some of the women stood with tears in their eyes.

"We are here," she heard Sarai whisper.

She was happy that she had the kind of friends who were always there for her and had no ulterior motives except to love and support her as she did for them.

"Richard, you need to stop!" she said, reaching for his arm.

He shrugged her hand off and continued his tirade, moving to stand directly in front of Nisha. Nisha's eyes followed him, staring him down.

"I had you and I have had my fill of you. You want to know something, Nisha? I even had a few of your so-called friends right under your nose. You remember your friend Tonya, who came to stay with us to help you after your surgery?" he said.

His eyes stared daggers at Nisha.

"I had her, more times than I can count, and sometimes even on the same day that I had you. Unlike you, she knows how to work what she has even with her fat self. Every time you left the house and every time you went to sleep before we did, that's what we were up to. You remember that time you caught me coming out of her room and I told you I was bringing her a comforter because it was so cold? That was one of those times."

He plowed on without a response from Nisha.

"You thought you were so clever but you couldn't even see what was happening right under your nose!" he said, his voice getting louder.

Victoria felt nauseated listening to the man she had just pledged her entire life to. Richard continued his rant, literally foaming at the mouth, walking around Nisha, who stood as still as a statue.

"I even had her in our bed. You think so highly of your so-called friends but even they don't genuinely care about you. You're just a means to an end for them, because they think you have access to my money!"

He pounded his chest as he said it.

"Truth be told, I could have had any of your friends if I wanted...but some of them were just too fat and ugly. I don't have a problem being a dog and getting notches on my belt, but even dogs don't bark at everything. Some of them were not even worth me taking my pants off. The lot of you are nothing special! Just faces and bodies to me. What do you think was going to happen with you showing up here? That I would leave Victoria for the likes of *you*? You meant nothing to me when I met you and you don't mean anything to me now. You were a means to an end. You work in a place where I needed information and I used you to get what I wanted. Now that deal has been finalized. You are as disposable to me as yesterday's trash. I got what I wanted and now it is time to move on from you."

"Richard, you need to stop! That is uncalled for!" Sean said, stepping in between him and Nisha.

Sean got into Richard's face.

"That is no way to talk to a lady, especially in a public setting like this! You're bugging, dude. Have you lost your mind?!" Sean asked, staring him down.

"That is no lady!" Richard spat back at Sean and pointed to Nisha. "She's no lady! She is nothing but a two bit wh—"

"Richard!" Sean interrupted him before he could finish his sentence. "Dude, quit! You are way out of order and out of bounds."

Sean grabbed Richard's arm and pulled him away from Nisha.

Victoria glanced at Nisha and her heart broke. All the color had left her face. Her eyes were cold and empty. Victoria had never seen anyone with that expression in her life.

"You know what, Richard?" Nisha said coldly. "That is absolutely true! People like you never suffer for what they put others through."

She spit fire and her voice rose as she walked toward him.

"You guys are like cockroaches when everyone else around is dying and suffering, the ones that deserves the most keep on living, unfazed and unbothered. It sometimes feels like there is no God that pays attention to the things y'all do. It seems like you guys are rewarded for being evil, while the good people die in the shadow of the pain, hurt and damages that you cause."

She went on, coming closer still.

"You said you made me? You wish you had. It's only little boys in men's bodies who perpetuate the lies that you do. You try to make others feel small so you can feel good about yourself. Always needing someone to stroke your tiny ego, so you would feel like a man. You're no man! You are a little, spoiled brat trying to convince people that you are good, but everyone knows you are a narcissistic, deplorable piece of scum. Gum under my shoe is better than you!" Nisha spat sneeringly at Richard.

"I am only responsible for my behavior, not for any shady friend pretending to care for me while screwing you on the side. Every dog has its day, and they will get what is coming to them. What goes around comes back around but on the second wave it is more savage than what I have faced and endured because of you. Today is my day to be embarrassed and suffer, but whoever I have done good to and have repaid me with evil will get their comeuppance in due time. Karma is a real thing and I know they will get it worse than I have."

She spoke bitterly, her eyes ice-cold.

"Today, however, is your day of reckoning, I promise you. You will never get the chance to make another person feel the way you made me feel."

The hairs on Victoria's arm stood up. Nisha reached into her pocket book and pulled out an 8mm handgun.

She pointed it at Richard, and said frostily, "Congratulations, you lying, dirty bastard," and squeezed the trigger.

For I know the plans I have for you," declares the Lord,
"plans to prosper you and not to harm you, plans to
give you hope and a future.

Jeremiah 29:11

CHAPTER 26

"No!!!" Victoria screamed and sat up in bed. Her nightgown was soaked and she was breathing heavily.

The man lying next to her sat up.

"Victoria, everything is okay? You were just having a bad dream. You are okay, hun. It is just a dream."

He brought her to his bare chest and wrapped her tightly in his arms. He kissed the frontal lobe of his wife and held her close. She fit perfectly as she always did, but he could feel her shivering with fear.

In the years that they have been married, this was the fourth time she had woken up like this, and he figured he knew why. He knew his wife well — sometimes, he thought, more than she probably knew herself. She was an open book to him and never hid her thoughts and heart from him. He knew when she was happy and sad. He knew what had caused her this nightmare. It happened around this time every year.

He kissed her lips and Vicky sighed. She ran her fingers along his flat abs and allowed her breathing to slowly return to normal. All thoughts of the nightmare and sleep were forgotten as she heard the quick intake of breath.

"I love you, babes," she said and pulled his mouth to hers.

He knew she did, and he was planning to show her how much he loved her right back. He kissed her deeply, drawing his finger over the silky skin he could never get enough of. She purred and Nicholas smiled.

He remembered the sound of the gunshot, and his mad dash back toward the church. He had to fight against the people that were trying to get out of the sanctuary. He had pushed through the crowd coming down the stairs like the woman with the issue of blood on her way to Jesus. No one was giving ground and he had to fight hard to get there. When he pulled open the door of the church, at least ten feet from him a small group of people were gathered. The first thing that he noticed was the bright red splashes all over. It took a minute for his mind to register that it was blood. He searched the faces, trying to find the one that mattered most to him. His eyes made contact with his sister Sarai. She was being held tightly by a gentleman he didn't know. Her head was on his chest but her face was toward him. She was crying hard. His heart dropped. Sarai did not cry much and, when she did, it was for good reason. He moved closer. Someone stepped aside to make room for him and that was when his world stopped.

Victoria was on the floor, her head on Richard's chest. She was covered in blood. He didn't know if she was hurt or not, her hand and face was covered and she was still. He saw her move and Nicholas realized that he had stopped breathing. Nicholas' lungs burned for oxygen and he took a deep breath. Richard moaned and Nicholas saw her hands move to check his eyes. Victoria had wanted to be a doctor but had let go of that dream just to survive in New York, but she had kept up on her CPR training. She had her hand pressed against Richard's stomach. Nicholas deduced that was where he was shot. Lying next to Richard was a young lady that Nicholas did not recognize. She was lying in a pool of blood, not moving. From where Nicolas was standing it seemed that the lower half of her face was missing.

Victoria looked up and saw Nicholas. Their eyes made contact and his heart skipped a beat. She looked at him intently, searching his face and the tears started flooding down her face. It broke his heart to see her crying.

"Are you okay?" he mouthed, moving closer to the circle of people. She nodded yes and returned her attention to Richard who was moaning in pain.

"You are going to be okay, Richard," he heard her say. "Help is on the way."

The words had barely left her mouth when the doors of the sanctuary flung open and the EMS team hurried in. They quickly assessed the situation and took over from Victoria. She explained that he was shot twice in the stomach and watched them take Richard away. His friend Sean went along with him. Police officers flooded the building, getting statements from everyone. A white sheet was placed over the body of the young lady. It was soon saturated with blood.

Nicholas stayed very close to Victoria, making sure she was okay. She started shivering and he took off his jacket and wrapped her in it. It was twice her size and she looked so tiny in it. He promised right then and there that He would always be there to keep her safe. He almost lost her today, not for any fault of her own, but still he wanted to make sure that everything was right in her world.

Richard had survived, with little to no evidence of the trauma he had faced. He seemingly had not learnt anything from his experience and was back to his old ways in a matter of months. Victoria had the marriage annulled. After the fiasco that had happened at the wedding, she wanted nothing to do with him. She didn't want to be involved with someone that lived their life in lies and deception, trying to get as much as they could without consideration for others' feelings. Nicholas made sure that he was there to support her during her recovery period. He had told her about his love for her, but she needed some time to heal after all that she had been through. He told her to take all the time she needed. After a year of counseling and therapy, she was ready for him to be a part of her life. Three months later they got married.

He loved this woman more than life itself and was extremely grateful and thankful that God had brought her back to him. He was getting a second chance and he had no plans of wasting one more day of his life being a fool.

As Nicolas drank from her lips, Victoria moaned in pleasure. He fully comprehended Songs of Solomon chapter 1 and verse 2, *"Let him kiss me with the kisses of his mouth: for thy love is better than wine."*

Whenever he drank from his wife's lips, he felt like a drunken man. He could never get enough of her taste and she was as heady as wine to his senses. He never got tired of this sensation and taste. No other women held a candle to her, it was not even a thought to look elsewhere for the love that his wife gave to him.

He had heard once you marry, women start throwing themselves at you, but he never gave it any thought until it happened to him. One month after he got married, women started making suggestive comments at him about wanting to be with him, even though he wore his ring with great pride. He never left home without it. Yet, they seemed to give no regard to that. Those brazen enough would say it could be "our little secret." When he was up late at night working, women he had not spoken to in months would DM, looking to have conversations. He never entertained them, always shutting them down immediately. He did not want to give any room for the enemy to come in and wreak havoc in his marriage. He kept no secrets from his wife. She had access to all his devices and knew his passwords, and was free to access them at any time. She had never requested that he do this for her, but after what she had gone through with Richard, he knew honesty and transparency was crucial to her sense of well-being.

Victoria had kept herself for him, and Nicholas was making sure that the gift of love-making was as satisfactory for her as it was for him. He rained kisses down her neck, stopping at her shoulder to take a nip on her satin smooth skin. Nicholas had a lot of women in his life, but the skin on his wife was to die for. He never felt such softness and silkiness on one person. When he mentioned it to her, she would laugh it off and state that he was flattering her. His fingers itched to always touch her body. In public, he was always reaching for her and she never shied away from him. She would come into his arms unashamed. He kissed his way down to her breast and drank like a thirsty man that had happened upon an oasis. Solomon chapter 7:3 flashed through his mind. *"Thy two breasts are like two young roes that are twins."* Victoria moaned and writhed under Nicholas' assault on her senses.

Her cool tongue on his ear, made his blood boil and he felt his blood rush through his body as desire took control of him and flowed unrestrained. Nicolas quickly got rid of what little clothing Victoria was wearing. It was in these moments he felt like Solomon. *"Thou hast ravished my heart, my sister, my spouse; thou hast ravished my heart with one of thine eyes, with one chain of thy neck. How fair is thy love, my sister, my spouse! how much better is thy love than wine! and the smell of thine ointments than all spices! Thy lips, O my spouse, drop as the honeycomb: honey and milk are under thy tongue; and the smell of thy garments is like the smell of Lebanon. A garden inclosed is my sister, my spouse; a spring shut up, a fountain sealed."*

The scent of her arousal was heady to him as he kissed his way around, down and all over her body. Nicholas branded her with his lips in places only his eyes saw and hands touched. Victoria whimpered and her back arched off the bed trying to get closer to her husband. Her hands grabbed the sheets as sweet agony took over her body. Fine mist of sweat rose on her brow and body as her blood raced through her veins. She twisted and arched, trying to merge herself into Nicholas. She withdrew her hands from the sheets and wrapped them around Nicholas' muscled back. Her acrylic nails drew soft lines down his back causing him to shiver and his manhood stood fully at attention for her.

Her breath came in little gasps as Victoria straddled him and Nicholas sheathed himself within the warm moist depth of his wife's body. She fit him like a tight glove and Nicholas felt every move she made. Her cool tongue licked his left earlobe again. She suckled softly for a brief moment. Goosebumps rose all over his body. Ecstasy took over Victoria's body and she kissed her way across his shoulder and back into his neck. She inhaled deeply, drawing his scent into her nostrils and she moaned in pleasure. She kissed the side of his neck and then suckled softly. Nicholas knew his neck would later reflect tonight's passion as his wife kept up her exploration of his person. She never lost the rhythm in her hips and waist and he adjusted her body as the tempo increased. He took deep breaths trying to slow down. He wanted to ensure that she was fulfilled before he gave into his urges but Victoria rode the waves of their passion to heights that only Nicholas could take her and she brought him along with her. The sound of heavy breathing coupled with the moans of pleasure broke the stillness of the night. Nicholas held on to his wife's waist as she danced to a song that began thousands of years ago with a simple phrase "...and Adam knew Eve his wife."

They both exclaimed in ecstasy and came hurling back to reality, bodies drenched in sweat and each trying to catch their breath, reposing in the knowledge that the marriage bed is undefiled. Nicolas kissed his wife's soft lips and she smiled. She had waited a long time for the beautiful opportunity of love-making that was untarnished by fear, guilt or remorse. God had blessed her with a man after his heart, a man that loved her in the way a woman was to be loved. A man that cared for her with a passion that was rivaled by no other. A man in whose arms she was safe, and content. She never felt jealous or insecure because she knew Nicolas loved God more than he loved her and that was saying a lot because he loved her with a ferocity that made her feel blessed to be the recipient of it. She knew he would not do anything to hurt God. Therefore, she rest assuredly in that love. She had sought God as Matthew 6:33 had admonished her to do and now everything she desired, prayed, cried and fasted for was being added unto her. She was very cognizant that many people were waiting and had been waiting for many years for the blessing she was enjoying. Therefore, she was grateful on a daily basis for the blessing she had received in the form of Nicholas.

Victoria smiled and placed her hand on her tummy. Psalms 139:13-14 came to mind and she repeated it softly as she gently stroked her tummy and listened to Nicholas' soft snores. *For you created my inmost being; you knit me together in my mothers womb. I praise you because I am fearfully and wonderfully made; your works are wonderful, I know that full well.* She was extremely excited and it was becoming quite difficult to keep this secret to herself. She told Nicholas everything; however, this - she wanted to keep to herself for a little bit and to ensure that it was at least a month in before she shared. Next week would make that month. Her plan to reveal this to him was already on the way, and she smiled in the darkness as she thought of what his reaction would be. She knew he was going to lose it. He loved children so much and had always maintained that he would never bear children with many different women. It had to be with one person. He wanted them to understand the concept and value of family, that is why even when he was a player, he took extra protection to ensure that no one trapped him into a loveless relationship.

She continued to caress her stomach thinking about the day that she found out. She had gone to the doctor thinking she was coming down with the flu because of the constant chills and the fact that she was unable to keep food down for the last week. The doctor ran some tests and took blood. She was behind on her physical for the year, so they were killing two birds with one stone to ensure all was okay. That afternoon, he had called her with the great news.

"Mrs. Parker, this is Dr. Lewis. We got back your results from the tests done today and I have some great news for you."

"Oh, that was fast," she said, placing the phone in the crook of her neck as she shuffled papers around on her desk, trying to find the report.

"Yes, I had them expedited to ensure all was well," Dr. Lewis said.

"Thank you for always looking out for me, Doctor," Victoria said, smiling.

"That's my job," he replied, laughing. "Well, most of your tests came back negative. No flu or any other abnormality was found. However, one of your results came back positive."

Victoria's heart slammed into her chest and she forgot about the report she was looking for, listening intently to Dr. Lewis.

"Positive?!" Positive for what?"

Fear crept into her voice.

"There is no need to be afraid," Dr. Lewis stated in his fatherly voice.

It was one of the reasons she had made him her primary care physician so many years ago. He always knew how to relate to her and he had a fatherly way about him that made her trust him absolutely.

"On a hunch, I decided to run a blood test to check for pregnancy and, Mrs. Parker, you are positively pregnant. No pun intended," he said laughing. "From my deduction, you are approximately three weeks along."

She sat at her desk in absolute shock, her world spinning. She heard the far away voice of Dr. Lewis saying, "Mrs. Parker, are you there? Hello, Hello?"

"Yes! Yes, I am here. This is quite some surprising news. Thank you for letting me know."

"You are welcome, Mrs. Parker. Congratulations! I will send you an email soon for a great OBGYN, who will take great care of you and your baby."

"Thank you," Victoria said, barely being able to hang up the phone before the tears broke through.

She sat at her desk, worshipping and giving God thanks for choosing her to be a mom. They had planned to wait at least three years to solidify their marriage and ensure its foundation was strong before starting a family but it seemed that God had other plans. She reminded herself that He knew what was best for her. Therefore, if He was doing this, there had to be a good reason, and she was happy with His decree for her.

Victoria came back to reality as Nicholas made himself more comfortable in their king-sized bed. She looked over at her husband sleeping peacefully, and his chest rising and falling with each breath he took. Each day, she prayed for his protection, safety and long life. She didn't even want to think about what her life would be like without him. Even in his sleep, he kept his arm around her. She enjoyed the tangible way he loved her. Her heart leapt with joy looking at her husband, the one whose covering and protection she was under, the one to whom her heart belonged, the one to whom she submitted without reservation, forsaking all others, clinging to him. He was the one whose name she bore with immense pride. Nicholas always stirred these emotions within her, whether he was asleep or awake, because of the type of man he was – a protector, her lover and best friend.

She loved watching him sleep. It was during this time that the weight of the world and the responsibility of his job did not furrow his brow, and she saw clearly the kind of man her husband was. She stared at him wondering what part of him her child would possess. Whatever portion of her and him that God decided to bless their daughter with - she didn't know why she believed wholeheartedly that she was bringing a feisty, little princess into the world - she would be beautiful. She kissed Nicholas on the frontal lobe and he smiled in his sleep. She couldn't wait to see his reaction when she told him that God was going to enlarge their family. He was going to be a fantastic father. She was thankful, grateful and blessed that she waited for her Boaz. She was an extremely happy woman and looked forward to each day she spent with the man whose rib she was taken from and who her prayers personified.

EPILOGUE

Jason sat on the park bench, his elbows resting on his knees, clenching and unclenching his fist. He couldn't believe this was happening to him. He had scoured almost the entire city and he still couldn't find a job. This angered him profusely. He was a good hard worker, why couldn't people see that? The anger that he was feeling was causing him to sweat profusely. He clenched his jaw and pain shot through his face. He rubbed the right side of his jaw, hoping to alleviate some of the pain. His hand ran over the screws that held his artificial jaws together.

He had gotten his jaw shattered in an alley. He was minding his own business when this guy came from nowhere and attacked him, getting involved in business that was none of his. He didn't notice the guy running toward him until it was too late, and he was lying flat on his back. The guy had pummeled his face repeatedly with an axe-like fist and he was unable to defend himself. It was a David versus Goliath scenario in terms of size and he was David - the underdog. He had woken up in pain en route to the hospital, escorted by two police officers. He could barely see from the blood in his eye and his face was on fire. He tried to talk and realized that he was not able to move his jaw. He had lost all except one of the gold teeth that he had put in that week. He was still pissed about that money down the drain. No one paid for the injuries caused nor for the replacement of his gold teeth. After his surgery, the officers had the audacity to handcuff him to his hospital bed to ensure that he stayed put. He remained cuffed until they transferred him to the police station and then off to court.

It took him nearly six months to relearn how to talk properly. It took that length of time due to the wires and screws in his jaw that limited his jaw's movement. He now spoke through his teeth like Fifty Cent, the rapper. However, unlike Fifty, he didn't have all that money to make him appealing to the ladies. His sex life was non-existent. Prior to this incident it was difficult, nearly impossible to get any booty. Even the skanks didn't want to have anything to do with him. It didn't help that he now had a rap for rape thanks to that highfaluting heifer from the club.

After he was well enough to attend court, his bail was set at $200,000 for assault and attempted rape. He didn't have that kind of money nor did anyone in his family. So he was incarcerated until sentencing. He was finally sentenced to five years behind bars. His lawyer, who was provided by the state, said it was fortunate that he didn't get much more and this was all because the girl he "supposedly" attacked never showed up at the hearing. The couple who rescued her that night and messed up his face came and told all sorts of lies about him. They told the court that the girl was resisting and fighting back, and he saw the assault on her person.

He tried to explain to the judge that it was a misunderstanding – the young lady was his girlfriend and they were trying to take advantage of the empty alley for a quickie. She liked rough sex and he was trying to accommodate her, as a good boyfriend does, when the couple showed up and interfered with their lovemaking. He didn't understand why the judge didn't believe him and sentenced him to five years. Could you believe that? You got sentenced to jail for making love to your girl in public? Was there nothing sacred anymore?

Jason sat back against the bench and took deep breaths in, trying to control his emotions. He had seen this form of anger management on YouTube and had been practicing to keep his emotions in check. His emotions, especially his anger, ruled him, and, oftentimes, when he got upset, all he saw was red. Most times, he was unaware of the damage he had done until much later. Most days, the breathing exercises worked. But, today, he was having trouble concentrating. It had been four months since his release. His mom took him in after he got out but she was demanding he pull his weight around the house this time and pay for half of everything or he would have to find somewhere else to live. She had done her share in raising him. He was a grown man of forty and she would not be putting up with his lazy and unproductive lifestyle anymore, she said. He needed to find a job fast. However, after his stint in jail, it was proving to be quite difficult to find work.

He was sitting in the park trying to work up the courage to go to the restaurant across the street and ask if they needed someone to clean up in the kitchen. All day long, he had heard 'no.' He didn't know if he could take another 'no' before he lost his cool completely.

Jason got up and headed toward the restaurant, as he waited for the light to change. He caught sight of two ladies walking to the door. As one of the ladies swung open the door, and held it for her friend who was laughing, his breathing slowed, his heart did a somersault and then began beating rapidly. He could not believe his eyes. There she was. The girl from the club and the alley. He would never forget her, not that smile. She was more beautiful now than he remembered. Time had been good to her. She looked amazing.

The white denim onesie that she wore hugged her curves like a second skin and highlighted her beautiful tan. Her orange toenails peeked out from the gold roman style sandals that she wore. Her hair was parted down the center and pulled back in a bun at the nape of her neck. Pancake size gold hoops swung in her ears as she tilted her head and laughed with her girlfriend as they entered the restaurant.

Her burst of laughter and happiness shattered something in Jason and his anger bubbled in him. She was the reason he was in this position. She was why all was wrong in his world and why he had spent five years in jail. She was the reason the girls didn't want him. He clenched his jaw in anger and he welcomed the pain as it fueled his anger. He hurried across the street and stood at the window looking in. He saw the ladies being seated and his anger rose. He clenched and unclenched his fist. That night in the alley, he swore he would make her pay, and he was going to keep his promise. Wherever she had been for the past five years, he was going to make her regret that she had come back to New York...

Made in the USA
Middletown, DE
09 July 2023

34771813R00146